CW01648077

LINDA DODDS

SHABBY WEDDING

The true story of Mary Jane Dodds,
“Married twice, buried twice and both her husbands hung

Mereo Books

2nd Floor, 6-8 Dyer Street, Cirencester, Gloucestershire, GL7 2PF
An imprint of Memoirs Books. www.mereobooks.com
and www.memoirsbooks.co.uk

Shabby Wedding

ISBN: 978-1-86151-585-8

First published in Great Britain in 2021
by Mereo Books, an imprint of Memoirs Books.

Copyright ©2021

Linda Dodds has asserted his right under the Copyright Designs and Patents Act 1988 to be identified as the author of this work.

A CIP catalogue record for this book is available from the British Library.
This book is sold subject to the condition that it shall not by way of trade or otherwise be lent, resold, hired out or otherwise circulated without the publisher's prior consent in any form of binding or cover, other than that in which it is published and without a similar condition, including this condition being imposed on the subsequent purchaser.

The address for Memoirs Books can be
found at www.mereobooks.com

Mereo Books Ltd. Reg. No. 12157152

Typeset in 11/15pt Century Schoolbook
by Wiltshire Associates.
Printed and bound in Great Britain

Acknowledgements

I would like to thank the late Mary Watson (*née* Dodds) for alerting me to this fascinating story, my husband Ian Dodds for accompanying and encouraging me along the way, and Susan Robson, Catherine Yates and my daughter Heather for their patience and valuable comments reading and re-reading the manuscript. I would also like to express my gratitude to Joy Walker for her generosity in sharing her own research, and my thanks to editor Chris Newton for all his help and guidance, along with everyone at Mereo Books.

By the same author

Blind Courage: the story of my father David Ronald Johnston, 1924-1976.

Mereo Books 2017

Author's note

I discovered the intriguing story of Mary Jane Dodds whilst researching my husband's family tree. The Dodds family, originally from Northumberland, were from the beginning of the nineteenth century renowned edge-tool makers in the small village of South Bedburn in the south west of County Durham. This in itself was of interest, but a conversation with Ian's elderly aunt sent me in a totally different direction. According to Aunt Mary, there had been someone within the family who had been 'married twice, buried twice and both her husbands hung' ('hanged' would have been strictly correct, of course).

From this startling statement, passed on as almost an aside, we went on to discover the amazing and tragic story of the lives and deaths of Mary Jane and Matthew James Dodds, who had lived in Hamsterley, a neighbouring village to South Bedburn, around a hundred years previously. It was a story that would not only shock the local inhabitants but make newspaper headlines both locally and nationally and catapult this small rural village into the spotlight for several weeks in the opening decade of the twentieth century.

My research meant hours scouring parish registers, births, marriages and deaths certificates, census returns, newspaper reports, court proceedings and much more. I have kept as close as possible to the facts, but you will, I hope, allow me a little poetic freedom to put some meat on the bones of the story where appropriate. Any inaccuracies or mistakes are completely my own.

The events took place in the small village of Hamsterley, which is an ancient village in the south-west of the County of Durham on a rise that overlooks the upper reaches of the Wear Valley. The River Wear rises high in the North Pennines and winds its way through a green and fertile valley before finally flowing into the North Sea at Sunderland. Of course, the name of the village has nothing to do with hamsters; it comes in fact from the word "hamstra", which was the old English name for a corn weevil that chomps its way through crops and plants. The syllable "ley" on a place name usually indicates a clearing in a wood, so the village is the clearing where the hamstra was found.

The nearest town is Bishop Auckland, famous for being the home of the powerful Prince Bishops of Durham; Auckland Castle was, until recently, the residence of the Bishops of Durham. Hamsterley has its own claims to fame. In the eighteenth century it was the first place in County Durham to grow potatoes, which became the main source of income for many of the village families. Then in 1872 the Backhouse family, Quaker bankers from Darlington, built Dryderdale Hall on the edge of the village, subsequently used as a location in the 1971 film "Get Carter". The village is bordered by Hamsterley Forest, which was established in 1927 when the Forestry Commission, set up after the First World War to tackle the timber shortage that had hampered the war effort, bought 4,000 acres of woodland. More recently, it appeared in a 2008 episode of the Channel Four TV series “Time Team”, which examined a nearby large stone structure known as the Castles, found to date from the late Iron Age.

Unlike the present-day village, the records from the 19th century show Hamsterley to be a poor community with many of its houses poor and decaying. A well-known rhyme from the time refers to the village in the line “Hamsterley Hungertown stands on a hill.”

For a village of its size, Hamsterley is well served by places of worship. The Anglican church of St James is rather unusually situated about half a mile east of the village. It was founded in the sixteenth century but possibly incorporates a much earlier church, there being a twelfth century Norman doorway. The building was renovated in the 1860s. The ancient little Baptist church was opened in 1715 and was one of the first dissenting chapels built in the North of

England. The Primitive Methodist Chapel in Hamsterley was built between 1884 and 1887, replacing an earlier chapel, and is a part of the Bishop Auckland and Shildon Methodist Circuit. The original village school, built in 1822, was next to the village green, but the building is now a well-used village hall and community centre and there is a new primary school behind the main road through the village.

South Bedburn is a small village, a hamlet really, sitting alongside Bedburn Beck, a small tributary of the River Wear, which has its origins high on Woodland Fell. Unlike its neighbour Hamsterley, Bedburn flourished in the 19th century, its farmers enjoying the security provided by copyhold tenures under the Bishops of Durham. For many years there was a large mill adjacent to the beck which had been used over the years for bleaching linen and forging edge tools, as a saw mill and for manufacturing stockings. It stood derelict for many years before being finally demolished. Today Bedburn provides the main entrance to Hamsterley Forest for tourists, hikers, mountain bikers etc. In 1858 South Bedburn is recorded as having a population of three hundred, but present-day numbers are much smaller.

However, in the late nineteenth and early twentieth centuries the village of Hamsterley was much smaller than it is today. Back then everyone knew each other, with many families having lived and worked in and around the village for generations. On the whole it was a poor village, the census returns indicating that the residents for the most part were working in manual jobs; miners, farmers labourers, coke drawers, labourers etc.

As in all small villages, life tended to revolve around the church, the village shop and the village public house. The glue which held the community together, as in all communities, was gossip; not of the malicious or malevolent kind, just the continuous passing on the everyday business of everyone else. No one was immune to it or exempt from it; every word, movement and activity of every village resident was faithfully noted, reported and commented upon over walls, across doorsteps, on street corners and over cups of tea. This continuous commentary on the affairs of the village constituted the only relief from the endless drudgery of daily life.

The closed mentality of the village people meant that its residents rarely ventured far outside its boundaries. The women would occasionally make a special trip into Bishop Auckland, where they would spend a morning at the market whilst their menfolk took their livestock to auction.

Chapter 1

It was into the close-knit, insular community of Hamsterley that Mary Jane Fatkin was born in 1853. She was baptised in St James' Church on the eleventh of September the same year. She was the only surviving daughter of William and Elizabeth Fatkin, nee Hodgson, their first daughter also bearing the name of Mary Jane, having died in infancy the previous year.

William Fatkin was born in Wolsingham in 1826, the son of a farmer. After working on the land from a young age, by the time of Mary Jane's birth he was employed as a coke drawer, a hard and dirty job which involved scraping out the coke from the bottom of a beehive oven using an iron rake and often his bare hands. Any foreign matter such as slate or slag had to be removed before the coke could be loaded onto the waiting carts.

Mary Jane attended the village school and received a typical, if limited, education for a girl of the times. She was in fact a product of her age, her main education being obtained in the home, helping her mother with the continuous round of cleaning, washing, ironing and cooking. Although in wider society things may have been changing and prospects for women to receive a higher education and enter into professions which had previously been reserved for men were increasing, such liberal ideas and attitudes had not yet reached rural south-west Durham. For Mary Jane, and young girls like her, life offered the prospect of little more than it had done for her mother and her mother before her; marriage, a family and a home of her own.

If Mary Jane did have any dreams of escaping the claustrophobic life of the village and the future predestined for her they seem to have been just that, dreams. Because on the 14th of December 1875, aged twenty-two, Mary-Jane married her neighbour, John Marquis, known as Jack, a man almost ten years her senior, in St James' Church. Jack came from generations of farm workers; his father, also called John, and his older brothers all worked as agricultural labourers. As such their lives were hard, and they worked long hours for local farm tenants in all weathers and for poor wages.

As a boy, Jack, like many boys in rural areas, skipped school to help with planting potatoes in the spring and harvesting in the autumn, and it seems possible he was destined to follow in his father's and brother's footsteps. However, by the age of fourteen, he and his elder brother Joseph had left home and were living and working with their uncle, John Stephenson, who was a grocer in the village. Presumably this involved starting at the bottom, sweeping the floor, scrubbing the counter, filling the shelves and barrels, unloading the delivery carts, weighing, measuring and dispensing.

Ten years later the brothers had moved on. Joseph, married by this time, had a shop of his own and Jack was living and working alongside him. By the time of his marriage in 1875, aged thirty, Jack had taken over the shop next door to the Cross Keys after the death of his brother Joseph and was well established as a grocer and the owner of several houses in the village. This was seen to be a good match for Mary Jane, providing her with a life that would be both secure and comfortable. She moved next door into Jack's house adjacent to the shop, which was set back slightly from the main road through the village and had an archway with large wooden doors leading to the back lane which separated the backyard from a row of ashpits.

Mary Jane would catch up with the latest village gossip from the customers who frequented the shop. Typical of small village shops, it was the epicentre of all the village tittle-tattle. With every slice of bacon cut, every quarter of tea-leaves dispensed and every bag of broken biscuits filled, the day's snippets of village news, scandal or just mere speculation were delivered, cogitated over and judgement passed. Against the backdrop of the delicious aroma of ground coffee mixed with mature cheese and smoked bacon, the minutiae of the village's existence were laid bare.

Occasionally someone might return from a visit to nearby Bishop Auckland with stories of the scandalous goings-on in the town, or news of a local tragedy would shock the village, such as the time when a millstone shattered, killing a young local lad. News from the outside world also grabbed people's attention from time to time, but such things were considered to be beyond their concern or experience and the conversation would quickly revert to matters closer to home.

Jack was able to provide well for his young wife, although the marriage remained childless. They enjoyed being a part of the social happenings of the village, such as at Easter, when spring clothed the village green in swathes of daffodils. Following the Easter Sunday service in St James' the villagers would gather to watch the children bowl their paste eggs down grassy slopes and challenge each other to 'jarping' contests where they smashed their boiled eggs together. Afterwards they would spread blankets on the green to eat their picnic teas in the warm spring sunshine.

The first weekend in August saw the annual Hamsterley Hoppings, when the windows of shop would be decorated with bunting. Jack and Mary Jane would join the crowd watching the traditional cricket match played on the green between the men folk of Hamsterley and a team from a neighbouring village. They would gasp as athletic young men attempted to climb a pole smeared in grease or cheer on the contestants in the wrestling contest, and Jack would take his turn to "hoy" horse shoes at a metal spike in the quoit pitches set up on the village green. There was a great deal of fun and laughter and the weekend would result in a marked increase in the shop's takings.

On the whole, the early days of their marriage appeared to have been relatively happy. Mary Jane was content with her life, and for the most part their life together was equitable. However, Jack was to appear in the Bishop Auckland Magistrate's Court on two occasions, firstly in 1877 and then again in 1880. He liked to go out most nights for a drink, usually frequenting the public houses in the village but occasionally visiting neighbouring villages. One such occasion was the evening of January the 23rd 1877, when Jack and his schooldays friend John Dodds from nearby Bedburn spent a convivial night in a public house in the village of Witton-le-Wear before setting off at about 9.30 pm to walk home. Their journey took them over Witton Bridge and up Crakehill Bank and they were just passing St James' Church on the outskirts of the village when they were set upon by three young ruffians. The two friends were knocked to the ground and cowered helplessly as they were violently kicked and robbed of what money they had in their pockets along with their hats and a stick.

Battered and bruised by the incident and severely shaken, they made their way to the village, where they reported what had happened to PC William Cruikshanks. However, as it was dark at the time, they were unable to give accurate descriptions of their assailants. Despite this the constable, assisted by his brother Alexander, who was a local sergeant, and another police constable named William Hutchinson, was able to apprehend the three attackers in the village of Etherley. They were brothers John and Michael McEleavey and John Sparks, who also went under the name of Etherington. As neither Jack Marquis or John Dodds were able to identify their attackers when the case came to court and despite the stolen property being found at the McEleavey's house, the JP, Reverend George Wilkinson, ruled there was insufficient evidence to send the prisoners to trial and they were discharged.

To further supplement their income Jack and Mary Jane had taken in two lodgers who occupied the spare bedrooms: John Coulthard, a widower and retired blacksmith, and young George Lowson, who worked as a labourer at a nearby colliery. Next door, Mary Jane's mother also had a lodger, PC George Applegarth, the village bobby.

One morning in the summer of 1880, Jack was out of bed and dressed early, announcing to Mary Jane that he would be working in the shop that day. Once he had left the house, Mary Jane took the opportunity to spend the day with a friend who lived further down the village. About mid-morning there was a loud knocking on her friend's front door and the sound of someone calling her name. It was the young son of the landlord of the Cross Keys, who breathlessly informed her she was needed at home as Jack had gone mad.

Not knowing what on earth could have happened, Mary Jane grabbed her shawl and followed the boy back up through the village. As she neared the house, she could not believe the scene which met her eyes. Jack was marching towards her in the middle of the road, dragging a young boy behind him whose hands were bound together with rope. Running beside them was the boy's black dog, which every few yards jumped up and bit its terrified owner. The boy was screaming to Jack to stop, saying that he was sorry and that he wouldn't do it again.

Mary Jane recognised the lad as ten-year-old John Dove, who was known to everyone in the village. The unfortunate boy's father, Thomas, had been killed in a pit accident when the lad was just two years old and his mother had remarried, abandoning the boy to live with his grandparents at Dixon Carr, a farm just outside the village.

Quickly running over to Henry Rowell, Jack's apprentice, who was standing with a group of villagers watching the horrifying scene, Mary Jane grabbed the lad by the arm and spun him round, asking, "Henry, what on earth is going on?"

"It's Jonny!" Henry gasped. "Mr Marquis was through the back shop getting some more potatoes and when he came back into the shop, he caught Jonny stealing five pence out of the till." Apparently, instead of just clipping the boy around the ear and threatening to tell his grandparents, Jack had decided to make an example of the boy. He had tied the lad's hands together in front of him and was now parading him through the village for everyone to see. Mary Jane was horrified and ran after Jack, pleading with him to let the boy go and telling him that he had made his point.

The following Monday young John Dove, dressed in his Sunday best and visibly shaking, appeared before the magistrates at Bishop Auckland Courthouse charged with stealing five pence from Jack Marquis. Several people from the village were willing to speak on the boy's behalf, telling the magistrates of his unfortunate circumstances. They vouched for his previous good behaviour and described how the boy had been mistreated by Jack and been bitten eight or nine times by the dog. The members of the magistrates' bench were, however, of the opinion that Jack had only being doing his duty and sentenced the lad to be whipped with a birch rod. The punishment was carried out immediately by a policeman from Bishop Auckland police station. Mary Jane later learned that the boy's grandfather had also appeared before a separate court and was fined for offences relating to owning a vicious dog.

Following the verdict, Jack felt vindicated in his actions and refused to express any remorse or regret in regard to the horrific punishment inflicted on the boy for what had been a relatively minor offence. Mary Jane, however, was deeply troubled by what had happened and what she considered to be her husband's extreme actions. She was mortally ashamed of what Jack had done and avoided going into the shop or out into the street as much as possible. She spent more and more of her time in her parent's house, constantly anxious about what Jack might do next. It was becoming obvious to her that Jack was ill, and that his mood swings and unpredictable behaviour were clearly symptoms of some deeper problem.

In early January 1887, the north was subjected to severe snowstorms which left many of the roads around the village blocked. On January the 10th, Dr Browning Patterson, who lived in nearby Butterknowle, somehow managed to make the arduous three-mile journey to Hamsterley in order to attend to his surgery there. On arrival in the village, he left the horse and trap with his driver with instructions to walk the animal about to prevent it from getting too cold.

What happened next was reported in the *Teesdale Mercury* on January the 12th:

In turning, the animal hit its foot, causing it to plunge across the road into the gutter. It then backed across the road, driving the trap against a stone wall, overturning it and breaking off the shaft. The driver was thrown out on the road. Thus liberated, the horse ran at a furious rate down the village, the shafts dangling at its feet. The door of Mr John Marquis was standing open, and the horse ran into the house, knocking down Mrs Marquis and breaking her leg. The animal was secured and Mrs Marquis attended to by the doctor.

As time passed Mary Jane became increasingly aware of her husband's mood swings and his tendency to lose his temper when outraged by something he considered to be a social or moral wrong. Normally a passive and tolerant man when it came to household affairs, he would suddenly fly into a rage when reading in the newspaper of some local or national matter that did not agree with his own way of thinking. When a customer passed on to him news of a misdemeanour by someone in the village, it was not unknown for him to bang his fist on the counter in his rage. Mary Jane quickly learned therefore to avoid in their conversations anything which might inflame this side of her husband's nature.

She also began to notice other changes in her husband's behaviour, his anger and agitation becoming apparent as he seemed to find more and more things which displeased him. He often came home after a long day in the shop irritated by the continual gossip of the women and disapproving of it. He had had several assistants over the years, usually young girls from the village, and even had an apprentice, Henry Rowell, a hardworking, willing young man whose family farmed at nearby Wolsingham. None of these seemed to stay that long, and Mary Jane was beginning to suspect that this might have something to do with Jack's mood swings.

Increasingly there were times when he did not seem to have the energy or interest to go into the shop at all; instead he would spend his days simply sitting gazing into the embers of the fire. At such times his mood was black. He spoke very little and there was nothing Mary Jane was able to do which would lift him from the dark place he seemed to be in.

The hardest thing of all was trying to predict her husband's state of mind. There were days when he seemed better and he would go to work in the shop as normal. On these days Mary Jane would take the opportunity to busy herself with her housework and maybe visit friends in the village. When Jack was in one of his dark moods, however, she took to spending the days with her mother in the house next door. Sadly, her father had died in 1884 after suffering for seven years with epithelial cancer, but Mary Jane and her widowed mother found comfort in one another's company.

As time passed Jack's condition steadily worsened and he regularly spent long periods in a deep melancholy, refusing to eat and not sleeping. Mary Jane begged him to visit the local doctor, but Jack refused to accept that there was anything anyone could do to help him.

On the morning of the twenty-second of May 1891, Jack walked out of his shop and headed for his hayloft. Passing that way a short time later was neighbour William Coatsworth, a livestock auctioneer and a well-known character in the village. William had had several encounters with the law, including an incident ten years previously when he had been charged with assaulting PC Thompson, the Fatkins' lodger, with a stick in Jack Marquis' shop whilst the worse for drink. A few years later he was charged again, this time for conducting a sheep and lamb sale in the village without an auctioneer's licence, for which he was fined £25.

As William walked past, he became aware of

Jack's dog, which was barking and acting in a strange and agitated manner. William followed the dog to the gate of the hayloft, where it stopped, refusing to go any further, before running off down the village.

Hearing the sound of another dog barking in the hayloft, William ventured inside to find the dog running about amongst the hay. Calling out "Jack, what are you doing?" he went further into the hayloft to find Jack's lifeless body hanging from a beam by a rope which was wrapped seven times around his neck. When William carefully cut him down and laid him gently in the hay, he saw that his face had turned black.

An inquest was held on the next day, presided over by Thomas Dean, the Coroner for Darlington Ward. Mary Jane's mother Elizabeth spoke of how Jack had been feeling rather low recently and said he had been drinking heavily all that week. Jack may have had some business worries, and it was known that both he and Mary Jane indulged in drink. Perhaps he even resented the time his wife spent with her mother next door.

The Coroner recorded a verdict of "Suicide by hanging whilst temporarily insane".

Mary Jane was now left to face living in this small community with the considerable stigma which was attached to a suicide. Attitudes amongst the villagers were typical of the times; suicide, or self-murder as it was sometimes referred to, was seen both as a criminal act and against the teachings of the church. There was a taboo and a certain amount of fear around the subject, which meant communities and families tended to avoid speaking of it.

However, this did not still the tongues of the village gossips and poor Jack's tragic end was the subject of whispered conversations for many weeks. Mary Jane was aware of the looks of pity on the faces of those she met and that people crossed the street to avoid having to speak to her. John Coulthard, the old retired blacksmith, was so affected by what happened in the house that he did not return to his rented room, and George Lowson moved back to his home village of Lands.

Under the circumstances therefore, it seemed

sensible that Elizabeth should move in with her daughter. They rented one of the vacant spare rooms to George Henderson, another young miner. Jack's death meant that Mary Jane was now a woman of substantial private means, having inherited his rented properties in the village, along with the grocery business. But at the age of thirty-eight she was now a widow, and it seemed she was destined to spend the rest of her years living with the consequences of her husband's decision to end his life in such a tragic and morally unacceptable way. The respectable and comfortable life which had been taken for granted now lay in ruins, and she seemed destined for a lonely and bleak future.

On top of all this, Mary Jane also had problems in settling her husband's financial affairs. Three months after Jack's death, on the 22nd of October, she was forced to take action in the Auckland County against James Knaggs, a 47-year-old miner and father of seven children. who was also churchwarden and sexton at St James'. Knaggs owed her late husband £21.19s 10d for goods sold and delivered to him. Her solicitor, Mr Teale, agreed that the case should be referred to the Registrar. The case came before the court again in April 1892 and Mr Teale asked for a judgment, which duly gave £6 18s 9d to Mary Jane, with £3 15s costs awarded against James Knaggs, payable at 7s 6d per month. There followed an amusing exchange between the two solicitors with Mr J. T. Proud pointing out that the offices of churchwarden and sexton were not very lucrative at Hamsterley. Mr Teale responded, to much laughter in court, that four funerals at once was evidence of some business there.

Chapter 2

William Dodds was born in 1722 in Minsteracres, where he had served an apprenticeship as a blacksmith. Having moved to Bedburn, he had established an edge-tool making business, there being a plentiful supply of ironstone in the immediate locality, along with a supply of wood for charcoal. There had been a mill on the site since Roman times and the one leased by the Dodds family dated back to the beginning of the 18th century. It was a large building, four storeys high and built of local stone, and had previously housed a bleachery for the whitening of cloth and yarn. The mill race began high on the opposite valley side and ran down to a millpond by the road side. From there the water ran through a tunnel under the road to emerge crashing over the enormous millwheel, which drove the power hammer inside the building.

Willy Dodds, as he was known, married Ann Atkinson in 1798 in St James Church and together they raised four sons and four daughters in South Bedburn. In later life Willy became something of a well-known character both in Hamsterley and in the village of Merrington Lane, where he also had a small foundry. He was short and quite stout and known for driving a little flat cart using a long stick which he could separate into two halves which he used as walking sticks.

The business prospered and by the 1860s it had become a Limited Company. It was said that the shovels, hay spades and bread knives made at the Dodds forge were the best in County Durham and that their tanners' and curriers' tools, cork cutters and ship's carpenters' tools could be found in all parts of the county.

William died in 1862 in Spennymoor, aged 90 years. The business continued in the hands of his sons and grandsons until more modern methods of manufacture caused it to decline and eventually to close, taking with it a major source of employment for the surrounding area. There was subsequently a hosiery and a sawmill on the site and the former forge fell into ruins.

The Dodds family were Baptists and worshipped in the little Baptist church in the village, which dated back to the seventeenth century. The congregation was small and several members of the Dodds family, including William, had been elders at the church. The little graveyard at the rear held many gravestones bearing the Dodds name. William's grandson, Michael John Dodds, still lived in the village, working as a joiner, and was a prominent member of the same little Baptist church where his grandfather had been an elder. He and his wife Hannah were married in 1864 and together they had four sons and three daughters. Hannah died in 1893 and of their three remaining sons, George married and moved to Bishop Auckland to work as a miner, whilst Matthew James and Charles Henry lived with their widowed father in Hamsterley, Charlie working alongside his father in his little joiner's shop.

Matthew had been born with one leg a couple of inches shorter than the other and as a consequence he wore a large built-up boot and walked with the aid of two sticks. He was a short, broad-chested man with a shaggy dark brown beard, quiet and withdrawn, who kept himself largely to himself. In his schooldays the other children in the village had run after him calling out hurtful names such as "hopalong" and "pegleg", and as a result Matt, as he was generally known, had become very much a loner.

Matt had worked for some years at the Seven Sisters Pit, one of the many small pits and collieries around nearby Cockfield, owned at the time by the Seven Sisters Colliery Co. Ltd, and producing household coal. It was at the height of its production, employing forty men in total, but Matt's disability meant he was one of the ten employed above ground, most likely putting his woodworking skills to good use cutting and shaping the thick tree trunks which would be used as props in the pit as well as sharpening and honing the picks and implements used by the miners. He was known to be a good, honest worker, setting off from Hamsterley in the early hours to make the long and arduous journey on foot across Cockfield Fell for his shift and then home again. Often his journey was in the dark and in the winter months he had to battle against the harsh north-east weather, but he never missed a shift. Whenever he could, Matt would help his father and brother in the joiner's workshop.

Over the winter of 1903-1904, Mary Jane's mother, Elizabeth, became increasingly unwell and was eventually diagnosed as having pernicious anaemia. Despite her daughter's careful ministrations, she died at the beginning of February, 1904 and was laid to rest beside her husband in the churchyard. Nobody was quite clear as to how, but not long after this it became obvious to the villagers that Matt and Mary Jane were in fact "walking out" together. Matt had known Mary Jane all of his life, although she was several years older than him. Their families had been neighbours in South Bedburn; in fact Matt's uncle, James Dodds, had been a witness at Mary Jane's marriage to Jack Marquis.

The opinion of most of the villagers was that although this was indeed a strange pairing, Matt was a harmless enough fellow and that they were both probably lonely people so there was likely no harm in it. Many thought that Mary Jane had suffered long enough following Jack's death and that Matt too had been long enough on his own and so if he could find some comfort at this time of life, then good luck to him. So it was that the village became accustomed to the rather strange sight of the two of them walking together in the evenings, she in a long dark dress and woollen shawl, he in his collarless shirt and muffler, limping noticeably on his big boot.

Their courtship was short and on the twenty-fourth of June 1905, without telling anyone of their intentions, they drove to Bishop Auckland

and were quietly married in the Register Office there. They failed to completely avoid the attention of the village however, and when they returned to Mary Jane's house, where they were to begin their married life together, a small group of well-wishers were gathered outside to welcome them home. Suddenly three or four of the local children jumped out on to the path in front of them. Giggling and nudging each other, the children reached into their coat pockets and took out great handfuls of brown dock seeds which they then began to throw over the startled couple, calling out in sing-song voices as they did so: "Shabby wedding, shabby wedding!" Once they had used up their supply the children ran off into the village, leaving the bride and groom to brush the tiny brown seeds from Mary-Jane's bonnet and shawl and the rim of Matt's bowler. No one gathered outside the house on that happy day could possibly have known how prophetic the children's little song would turn out to be.

Each morning Matt made his rather laborious way over Cockfield Fell to Seven Sisters Pit, as well as continuing to help in his father's joinery shop, which occupied the corner site at the fork of the road which led off to Bishop Auckland. There he spent his time not only with woodworking but attending to the various needs of local farmers and tradesmen. It was a well-known fact that if you needed a blade of any kind grinding, then Matt was your man.

Now that he was married to a woman of property, Matt's skills were also put to work on the six cottages Mary Jane had inherited from her late husband. These were in various states of disrepair, suffering as they were from years of neglect, and Matt set to work repairing leaking roofs, rotten window frames and ill-fitting doors. It was obvious that he found satisfaction in the work, and the tenants were all appreciative of the quality of his workmanship. Occasionally Mary Jane would arrive whilst he was working and they would discuss together how the work was progressing.

Their evenings were spent quite amicably, with Matt reporting progress on the repairs to the houses and Mary Jane repeating any snippets of village gossip she had acquired in the shop that day. The evenings in the kitchen slowly became more strained however, and they spent increasing amounts of time in silence; Matt was not accustomed to making small talk. Their previously agreeable discussions in regard to the properties also began to take on a different tone as Mary Jane became more critical of the progress of Matt's work. He in reply voiced his growing belief that as it was his work which was giving extra value to the cottages, he should in fact have joint ownership of them.

This latter claim, based also on what he believed to be his rights as a husband, soon dominated Matt's conversations with his wife. She simply refused to discuss the matter any further, insistent that the cottages were hers by right and that Matt had no claim upon them.

One evening, things came to a head. Matt was in his usual place at the kitchen table, uncommunicative with his head behind the daily newspaper. Mary Jane sat opposite, the remains of their evening meal still on the table between them, her shoulders slumped and her face dark with temper. Without warning she sprang from her seat, slamming her chair against the wall behind her. Then, grabbing a jug from the dresser, she announced that she could bear it no longer and needed something to help her cope with the hell of her existence. At this she stormed out of the back door, slamming it resolutely behind her.

A short while later a still furious Mary Jane returned to the kitchen, the jug now containing a gill (a quarter pint) of beer, which she proceeded to drink in a sullen silence. Matt, apparently unmoved by this display of defiance, simply continued reading his newspaper without remark. The pattern was now set, however, and on most nights Mary Jane could be found knocking on the side door of the Cross Keys, her jug in her hand.

Chapter 3

A few days before the Christmas of 1906, it was reported by the customers in the shop that Mary Jane had been seen in the village with what appeared to be a black and swollen eye. The following morning Matt was working as usual in the joiner's shop when a customer, whilst waiting for his axe to be sharpened, casually commented that his wife had noticed the state of Mary Jane's eye. Matt just laughed, seemingly unconcerned: "Oh that" he answered, not taking his eye from the grinder, "It's nothing. Mary Jane lost her footing when she was stepping down from the trap and fell against the step. She's got a proper shiner!"

The new year was marked with a change of wind direction to the north, bringing night frosts and eventually snow. Villagers struggled to get around in the deep drifts and on the icy pavements. However, it began to become clear to those frequenting the village shop that once more, all was not well next door. Lizzie Longstaff, who lived a few doors away from the couple and was always an open source of information when it came to the comings and goings of the village, bowled into Mr Robson's shop one morning eager to share her news of an encounter with Mary Jane in the back street. Lizzie had just come out of her own gate to cross the little alleyway which divided the back yards from the row of ash closets when she had almost literally bumped into Mary Jane. The latter had obviously not wanted to stop to speak and had put her head down onto her chest in an attempt to sneak away unnoticed. Lizzie, however, was not the sort of woman to be easily avoided and she had made a point of blocking Mary Jane's path. Mary Jane had continued to hold her head down, trying to avoid eye contact, but Lizzie had insisted on engaging her in conversation.

It was then that she noticed it. "A black eye" said Lizzie, standing with both arms folded across her ample bosom. "As bonny a shiner as I've ever seen! Of cause she mumbled something about walking into a door, but I know what I saw. She has no more walked into a door than I have".

Lizzie's news certainly caused a stir. Tongues soon began to wag and word of Mary Jane's "accident" spread. From that day on, the couple's relationship became a regular topic of conversation in the village shop and in the Cross Keys.

A few weeks after the incident with the black eye, Alice Stephenson, wife of the landlord of the Cross Keys, was busy as usual serving jugs of ale and wiping down the tables when Mary Jane, swaying slightly on her feet, came into the snug. Pushing up the sleeve of her dress to above the elbow, she insisted on showing Alice some marks on her upper arm which to the latter looked remarkably like finger marks.

Not too long after that incident, another neighbour, local farmer Joseph Watson, returned home one evening to his wife and recounted how that morning he had taken a knife along to the joiner's shop for Matt to grind. While he was waiting for the job to be done, another man had come in on a similar errand. He appeared to be a friend of Matt's and engaged him in conversation:

"I've just seen your lass," he began, "she was on her way to collect some rents from them cottages of hers down the end of the village. That's a rare fat lip she's got mind."

"Aye," Matt answered, "happened yesterday. She was climbing up on the wall of the midden to get at the eggs. The bloody hens have taken to laying on the top. I've told her before to be careful, she's too old to be climbing walls. Came a right cropper she did. Blood everywhere."

As well as the mysterious injuries which Mary Jane seemed to have from time to time, there was also speculation about her drinking habits.

Although she could not be thought of as a drunk, her frequent appearances at the side door of the Cross Keys to ask Thomas Stephenson for a gill of beer or a shilling's worth of whisky were not going unnoticed. Not that this was particularly unusual – most of the local women did the same from time to time – but in Mary Jane's case it was the increased frequency of these visits and the odd times of the day they were made which was giving rise to village gossip. Since the death of her mother, it was now not unusual for Mary Jane to call at the side door of the Cross Keys two or three times in a day, occasionally even knocking on the door before nine in the morning.

One night, around midnight, the Robsons were wakened from their sleep in their flat above their shop by a commotion outside. Mr Robson opened the window to see Mary Jane outside in the street and Matt leaning out of an upstairs window, the two of them yelling and gesticulating at one another. When Mr Robson asked them to keep the noise down, Matt yelled across that his wife was refusing to come inside and Mary

Jane yelled just as loudly back, accusing him of "knocking her about".

Poor Mr Robson did not know what to do; by this time all his family were awake and wanting to know what was happening. As he needed to be up early the next morning to put up a big order, he yelled at the pair again, telling them that if they didn't sort themselves out quickly, he would have to call for PC Lowe.

Nothing, it seemed, would quieten the two of them, so Mr Robson was true to his word and sent one of his sons to fetch the local bobby. By this time Mary Jane was nearly hysterical and it was clear that, she at least, had been drinking. She let forth a stream of abuse at Matt, who was still hanging out of the bedroom window, calling him every conceivable name you could think of and mocking his disability. Matt retaliated, entreating everyone to listen to the sort of abuse he had to put up with every day.

When the policeman arrived, Mary Jane threw herself onto the pavement and pleaded with him not to make her go inside. She insisted that Matt had been mistreating her and that she no longer wanted to live with him. Poor PC Lowe was faced with having to reassure Mr Robson, who was becoming more and more anxious about the lateness of the hour, as well as calming Mary Jane down and persuading her to go indoors.

Finally he managed to extract a promise from Matt regarding the safety of his wife, but insisted that as a policeman there was nothing more he could do about the situation. He advised Mary Jane to see a solicitor.

Stories continued to circulate around the village of occasions when people had witnessed exchanges between the two. One morning Mary Blackett, wife of the village blacksmith, who lived in a little cottage on the edge of the village, had been on her way to Robson's shop to buy eggs when she passed the open door of the Dodds' house. "I was just passing when I heard a shout, well a cry really," she later reported to an enthralled audience in the shop. "Then I heard this almighty bang. I thought someone was in trouble, so I thought I'd better check. There was no answer, so I reckoned I'd better go in. There she was, Mary Jane, right in the middle of the kitchen floor, flat on her back, and the kitchen chair upturned beside her. I said, 'Are yer alright, Mary Jane, whatever has happened?'

"I helped her up on to the chair and I was just gettin' her a cup of water when next thing I know is, Matt comes rattling down the stairs. He went right up to Mary Jane's face and said to her, 'If you say anything more, I'll strike your bloody head off!' Then he pushed her onto the floor again and stormed out."

One afternoon not long after that incident, an excited Joseph Robson went into his father's shop bursting with news of what he had just seen in the back lane. "It's Mary Jane." he announced to the astonished customers, "Matt's locked her in the outhouse! I was just passing when their back door opened and Mary Jane ran out. Matt was chasing her; he had a broom and he was shaking it at her. Then he pushed her with it all the way into the outhouse and locked the door. She must like it though, cos I could hear her singing at the top of her voice!"

Many told of hearing Mary Jane taunting her husband about his disability, calling him names along the same lines as the children of the village had done but on occasion being much more vindictive. At the same time there were reports of Matt using bad and even threatening language against his wife. To most folk, it seemed that each was as bad as the other and in time nothing much was made of the matter. If shouts were heard outside, then customers in the shop or the Cross Keys would look at each other, shrug their shoulders and continue with their business. Even the sight of Mary Jane with blackened eyes or cuts and bruises became familiar and people would sympathise with her when she showed them marks on her arms or legs. The Stephensons at the Cross Keys became accustomed to opening their door to Mary Jane's knocking to find her slumped on the step, slightly merry, Matt having locked her out. Those who called in at the joiner's shop would regularly hear stories of drinking and taunting and shake their heads in sympathy. All agreed that Matt and Mary Jane's marriage was far from being a happy one.

Chapter 4

The Reverend John Holliday, Vicar of Hamsterley, lived in the large vicarage opposite the Cross Keys. One morning in early February 1907, he was working in his study when there was a loud knocking at the door and he heard women's voices in the hall. After a few moments his wife ushered a flustered-looking Mary Jane into the room. After settling her in the chair facing his desk, the Reverend asked what it was that he could do for her, and she explained that she wished him to witness her will.

As she was in possession of several properties

in and around the village and was approaching her fiftieth year, with a husband who was several years younger, the vicar did not feel this to be an unreasonable request. In fact, he was quite often called upon to write and witness the wills of people in the village. He carefully penned his name on the document in his scholarly, italic writing. The will stated that it was Mary Jane's wish to leave her entire estate to her husband Matthew James Dodds in the event of her death. On completion of the signing, a few minutes were spent in general conversation before the vicar showed Mary Jane out of the front door and with very little further thought, returned to his sermon writing.

He was surprised, therefore, when in August Mary Jane again appeared at his door and explained that she wanted to him witness another will. Once again, she was ushered into the vicar's study and seated in the chair opposite his desk. This second will stated that her husband, Matthew James Dodds, was to be entitled to only £40 and the rest of her property, with the exception of a couple of legacies, was to be left to her cousin Margaret Pattison, who lived in Bishop Auckland. Once again, the vicar signed the document as requested.

As the months passed, loud voices continued to be heard coming from the Dodds' house and on several occasions Matt's threats of "I'll bash your brains out!" were heard. William Henderson's daughter Edith returned home one afternoon saying that as she had passed the house the front door had opened and Matt, waving a sweeping brush in his hand, had pushed Mary Jane out onto the pavement shouting, "I'll kill you!" However, on the whole, the residents of Hamsterley paid little attention; after all, what happened between a husband and wife was their own business.

During the afternoon of February 20th 1908, Mary Jane was making one of her regular visits to the Cross Keys when she encountered George Marr, who had worked as an assistant in the village shop for several years, and was sweeping the pavement outside of the shop. They exchanged greetings before Mary Jane, huddled against the cold wind, continued to the side door of the pub, where she asked for a shilling's worth of whisky. Shortly afterwards, George was in the shop when George Waistell and a woman he knew to be called Braithwaite came in, saying they had heard particularly loud shouting and screaming coming from the Dodds' house.

Paying little attention at first, George continued with his work, but then he heard a voice, which he recognised to be that of Mary Jane, pleading: "Oh, dear, oh dear, dinnatt dee it!" This was repeated several times. The shouting and screaming continued for a full ten minutes and then there was a short silence before he distinctly heard the sound of a bolt being shot into the side door of the property. The shouting started again, the voice again being that of Mary Jane, but after another ten minutes or so all was quiet once more.

Shrugging to himself and presuming this to be one of the couple's regular arguments, George turned his attention back to his work. Later that same afternoon, the door to Robson's shop banged open and Matt, breathless and in a state of obvious agitation, asked George, who was standing behind the counter, if Mrs Robson was home. On being told that she was not, Matt turned quickly on his heels and hurried clumsily out of the shop and back through the archway which led to the rear of his house.

Sarah Jane Wade, who lived in the house next door, was awakened from her afternoon nap by a loud banging on her back door. Wearily she got up from her armchair and opened the door to find Matt on the doorstep in a very distressed state. "Sarah," he gasped, "will you come? Mary Jane's burnt to death!"

Leaving her door standing open, Sarah ran from the house and into her neighbours' house, through the kitchen to the open door of the sitting-room. The room was in darkness and it took Sarah a few moments to adjust to the lack of light. What she saw caused her to give an involuntary shriek and her hand flew to her mouth. Lying face down on the rug in front of the fireplace was Mary Jane, seemingly lifeless.

“Oh Matt,” whispered Sarah, “whatever has happened?”

Matt did not follow her into the room but stood in the doorway staring at the body of his wife. His face was completely drained of all colour and his arms hung helplessly by his sides. Gasping to get his breath and obviously struggling to control the shaking which was threatening to overcome him, and in a voice that was not much more than a whisper, he explained to Sarah that he had come home and found Mary Jane lying under the bars of the fire and had lifted her out and onto the rug.

“Come on, Matt” Sarah said quietly, “let’s see if she’s alive.”

Still Matt remained in the doorway, seemingly unable to come any closer. Sarah could see that Mary Jane’s clothes were still smouldering, so she patted the flames out using her bare hands, burning them quite severely as she did so. She then put her face close to Mary Jane’s, but there was no sign of breathing, and lifting her head a few inches off the floor, she noticed a trickle of blood running from Mary Jane’s mouth onto the hearth rug. Sarah then gently raised Mary Jane's limp arm into the air and let it fall back onto the rug. It was obvious there were no signs of life.

As she slowly stood up again, Sarah noticed that there was no fire burning in the grate and very few cinders, other than a few large ones lying on the fender, which seemed strange. Looking down at the poor woman's body, she could see that her clothes were almost entirely burned off, with only a small piece of her blouse remaining on her right arm, and she could just make out what appeared to be a shawl or something similar around her neck. Mary Jane's face was a dark colour and her neck seemed to be swollen up to just below her ear. Thankfully, Sarah thought, Mary Jane's face did not seem to be burned at all and there were no burns on her neck.

Snapping into action, Sarah turned and taking Matt's arm she steered him back into the kitchen. "Come on Matt, you'll need to send for the constable," she said. The post of village constable was a quiet one for PC Lowe; drunkenness and the occasional horse theft were the most serious crimes he had had to deal with so far. His evening meal was disturbed that day by a hammering on the door. When his wife answered it, she found Matt on the doorstep. He informed her that his wife had burned to death and would the constable please come.

When PC Lowe arrived a few minutes later, dressed against the cold of the night in his greatcoat over his regulation serge jacket, it was to find the back door standing open and no one apparently home. Cautiously the constable went into the house and into the sitting room to find the body of Mary Jane still lying on the hearth rug. Bending over the body, he quickly ascertained that she was indeed dead. Her face was a darkish blue colour and her lips swollen.

A noise in the kitchen alerted him to Matt's presence. Prompted by Sarah, he had been to the undertakers to ask him to make a coffin for his wife. PC Lowe took Matt through into the kitchen, where someone had lit a small oil lamp and placed it on the table. Seating Matt at the kitchen table, the constable took a notebook and pencil from his jacket pocket and began to question him as to how his wife had come to be lying where he found her.

Matt once again explained that he had found Mary Jane lying in the fire and had pulled her out onto the hearthrug. The constable then asked if she had been drunk that day, to which Matt replied that she had had some drink in the house and that she had earlier offered him a glass of whisky, which he had thrown into the fire. After a short pause, he added: "Aye, she was drunk".

After writing all this down in his notebook, PC Lowe then asked Matt if he had sent for a doctor, and as he had not, he suggested that he should send a telegram immediately. Doctor Cunliffe, who lived in nearby Witton Park, was entertaining some distinguished guests to dinner that evening, as it was his wife's birthday, so he was particularly annoyed to receive a telegram informing him of a woman who had burned to death in Hamsterley and saying his immediate attendance was requested.

He apologised to his guests and his wife for the interruption to their celebrations and made his rather unsteady way round to the back of the house, where he stabled his horse. Hence it was almost ten o'clock before he arrived at the Dodds' house to find a small crowd had gathered in the back lane despite the lateness of the hour. PC Lowe was waiting for him in the back street, and unlocking the door he ushered the doctor, still grumbling about the fact that he had been dragged from his celebrations, into the house.

The doctor and the constable went straight through into the sitting room, which was in darkness, the only light coming from a candle which the constable held. Carefully, Dr Cunliffe turned Mary Jane's body over on to her back to find a poker that had been lying beneath her, and on closer examination he discovered a cinder clasped in the dead woman's left hand. Noting the extent of her burns, the discoloration of her face and the swelling around her neck, the doctor affirmed to the constable that the probable cause of death was by burning.

After briefly stopping to pass a word of commiseration to Matt, the doctor left the house to return to his dinner party and his guests, while PC Lowe told Matt that he would make the necessary arrangements for an inquest. Matt quietly then asked if it could be held the following day. Once the constable had also left, Sarah then suggested that, owing to the lateness of the hour, Matt should spend the night at his father's house.

Chapter 5

The inquest was in fact held on the 22nd of February in the main bar of the Cross Keys and was presided over by Mr John Thomas Proud, solicitor and Coroner from Bishop Auckland, ironically the same man Mary Jane had faced in court over her claim against James Knaggs in 1891.The small room was crowded, all the tables and chairs having been removed. The villagers who had been summoned as witnesses were standing along one wall, shuffling their feet nervously and whispering to each other. The Coroner was seated behind a small table upon which he had placed a large ledger and into which he occasionally made notes in a slow, laborious hand. Matt, his face pale and drawn, was seated to his right, accompanied and supported by his father Michael and brother Charlie. The rest of the space was taken up with as many villagers as could squeeze through the door and the room buzzed with anticipation.

The Coroner banged impatiently on his table several times with a small gavel before successfully bringing the room to order. He announced that the purpose of the inquest was to establish the cause of the sudden death on the previous evening of Mary Jane Dodds. He then called the witnesses one by one – George Marr, Reverend Holliday and Sarah Wade – who each nervously related what they had witnessed of Mary Jane and Matt's movements the previous day, the shouting and screaming which had been heard coming from the Dodds' house and what had been discovered in the sitting room.

Matt was then called and sworn in before giving his version of what had taken place. Mr

Proud then questioned him about the accounts by the witnesses of shouting having being heard coming from his house and Matt flatly stated that they must have been mistaken, as there had been no shouting.

Thanking Matt, the Coroner then announced that he now intended to go and see for himself the scene of the tragedy, whilst everyone else was to remain where they were. The Coroner rose from his seat and went out of the of the pub and along the street to Matt's house, where he entered by the front door and proceeded into the sitting room, where he found Mary Jane's body still lying on the hearthrug. The Coroner lifted the sheet which had been placed over the body by Sarah Wade and knelt down beside it, taking note of the burnt clothing, the dark colouring on the face and the swelling around the neck. The Coroner then replaced the sheet and turned his attention to the fender and the hearth and the scattering of cold cinders on the floor. Duly satisfied that he had seen all that he needed, he took a quick glance around the room before leaving the house and returning to the pub, where he spent a few minutes writing notes in his ledger. Mr Proud then called the room to order once more and proceeded to pronounce his findings.

"This case, on the face of it, looks to me somewhat suspicious," he said. "It is a curious thing how this woman, even in drink, could manage to get within that fender and be literally burnt to death without making any effort to save herself and without any other inflammable things in the room catching fire. Consequently, I am recording an open verdict and will be instructing the police to make further investigations."

Mary Jane's death certificate, issued on the 25th of February, recorded the cause of her death as "Burnt to death but insufficient evidence to show how the burning was caused". Mr Proud then stated that he was releasing the body for burial, at which Matt slumped forward in his chair, placing his head in his hands.

Those present then offered their condolences to Matt before spilling out of the Cross Keys and into the road. Comments were made amongst the small groups who were making their way home about the matter of the shouting and saying that it was strange that neither the police constable nor Dr Cunliffe had been called to give evidence.

As was the custom, Mary Knaggs and Mary Liddle were then summoned to attend to Mary Jane's body, which had now been carried into the bedroom, and perform the traditional duties of laying her out. Whilst washing Mary Jane's face they discovered a shawl wound tightly around her neck, so tightly that the flesh of Mary Jane's neck was hanging over it. After unsuccessfully trying to remove it, Mary went down into the kitchen and fetched a pair of scissors and inserting her finger between it and Mary Jane's neck she carefully cut it away. They then gently washed the body and dressed her in a new white nightdress and laid her on clean bedsheets. Then, in accordance with the old superstition, they drew the bedroom curtains and covered the dressing table mirror. Just as they finished their ministrations, there was a shout from the room downstairs and the undertaker came up the stairs to take the measurements he required for the making of the coffin.

A service was held in St. James's and Mary Jane was laid to rest in the churchyard alongside her parents, Matt standing expressionless throughout and supported on either side by his father and brothers. At the end of the ceremony, he leaned over the grave, tossed a single rose onto the plain wooden coffin and walked slowly out of the churchyard. There was no wake, although a few glasses were raised to Mary Jane's memory in the Cross Keys that night.

Meggie Pattinson, Mary Jane's cousin, arrived at Matt's house following the service and on seeing her he simply said: "It's a bad job happened, Meggie."

"Yes, I suppose so," she replied, at which Matt broke down in tears.

Just then James Brown, a medical student who was staying in the village, came to the kitchen with a will which his brother had drawn up and was surprised to find that Matt was in possession of another will. Meggie Pattison was also surprised. She was aware of the will in Mr Brown's possession because Mary Jane had told her of it, but she knew nothing of this fresh will. Mr Brown read out both wills and pronounced that it was this latest will that bequeathed everything to Matt that would stand.

That, Matt thought, was that. However, on the evening of March the eighth, responding to loud knocking on his door he found Police-Sergeant Daley from Bishop Auckland who, after entering the kitchen, informed Matt that he was arresting him on suspicion of having caused the death of his wife. Showing little emotion, Matt replied: "Well, I can say this, I was not in the house when it happened, that's all." Sergeant Daley then asked Matt for the last will, which he produced from the dresser drawer and then, taking him firmly by the arm, he marched him out of the house.

Chapter 6

The police station in Bishop Auckland was in Bondgate, the oldest part of the market town, and had been erected in 1846. It was a forbidding, grey stone-faced building with a blue lantern hanging on a bracket over the main entrance and the single word "POLICE" carved into the stone lintel above the door. The building was made up of a large office and a smaller room into which prisoners were taken for questioning. There was also a single cell, measuring barely ten feet by ten, in the basement of the building, and this was normally occupied by one of the town's drunkards and petty thieves.

Matt sat disconsolately on the hard stone bench and stared ahead of him at the damp, tiled wall. The air in the cell was rancid, and the smell, a powerful reminder of its regular occupants, was almost unbearable. On the bench beside him was his untouched breakfast, which had been brought in as the first weak beams of light had filtered through the cell's only window high up in the wall; Matt had no stomach for refreshments. He had spent a sleepless night on the stone bench curled under a single, filthy blanket, his mind filled with the images and sounds of the last few days.

Suddenly the sound of the heavy bolt on the outside of the cell door being pulled back broke his reverie and the bulky form of Sergeant Daley filled the door space. In the semi-light Matt could just make out that he was holding a piece of paper in his outstretched hand:

"This is a warrant, just arrived from the Home Office," he announced in an officious voice. It was clear that he had never dealt with such a thing before. "It gives permission for the body of your wife, Mary Jane Dodds, to be exhumed from where it lies in the graveyard of St James's church in Hamsterley and for it to be taken to a suitable location where a post-mortem and further examination will take place."

Following a moment's hesitation whilst he established that the prisoner had heard this, he continued: "You are to remain in custody here in Bishop Auckland until the results of the examination are known, after which decisions will be made as to how your case will proceed."

At this the he slammed the cell door shut and rammed home the bolt. Matt remained as he was, motionless, his eyes staring straight ahead for several minutes before slowly curling up on the hard surface of the bench, his face tight against the stone of the cell wall.

When the news of the impending exhumation of Mary Jane's body reached Hamsterley, the village was thrown into a state of utter shock and frenzy; nobody could remember anything of this enormity ever happening in the village's long history. People gathered together in the shop, the Cross Keys and their private homes to talk about it, no one quite able to believe what was happening in their own little community. There were those who claimed to have always known that Matt Dodds had the potential to be a violent man, Mary Jane's unexplained injuries confirming their suspicions, and those who could not believe someone of Matt's quiet nature and good family could be capable of murder. The talk was of little else, the events of the past weeks being discussed, dissected and analysed over and over again.

The morning of the 10th of March was bitterly cold with a constant thin drizzle, but the weather did not deter a crowd of over a hundred men, women and children making their way from the surrounding district to stand with those from the village outside Hamsterley churchyard. Amongst them were reporters and photographers from the *Northern Echo* and *Auckland Times*, who vied with those around them to ascertain a position of the greatest advantage.

A group of men were standing at the gate of Hamsterley church, huddled against the wind and the rain and speaking in hushed, solemn voices. They were Sergeant Daley, Doctor Cunliffe, Doctors J Dickenson Leigh and Wardle from Bishop Auckland, and a Doctor Farquharson. Beside them was the Reverend John Holliday, who had been required to request the appropriate Faculty from the Diocese to allow the exhumation to take place and who was clearly in a state of great unease. The men were flanked by the Chief Constable, Mr Morant ,and three police constables, each wearing their thick black serge cloaks, helmets on their heads and heavy wooden truncheons in their hands.

Just behind them stood Bill Thompson holding the halter of a big Clydesdale which was hitched to his flat hay cart. He too seemed to be ill at ease. Further away was a significant body of police constables charged with keeping the assembled crowd at a suitable distance and from entering the churchyard.

Several minutes passed before the group of men began to slowly walk down the church path and around the outside of the church itself to stand beside the freshly filled-in grave of Mary Jane, on top of which were the few bunches of flowers left by well-wishers, now beginning to wilt. Waiting for them beside the grave and leaning on their shovels were the two sextons and two local farmhands, who in response to a slight nod from the Chief Constable began to shovel the damp earth from the grave onto a mat of sacking which had been placed to one side.

The assembled officials stood in respectful silence until the coffin was exposed and the sextons brushed away the soil from the brass nameplate. Then, accompanied by Reverend Holliday's quiet praying, the four men placed strong ropes through the handles and gently lifted it clear of the grave, handfuls of straw being then used to clean away the soil from the side of the coffin.

Once it was cleaned the men gently lifted it onto their shoulders before walking slowly and respectfully back along the church path, followed by the official party and with Reverend Holliday still praying softly, until they reached the waiting flat cart upon which they placed the coffin. Bob Thompson then encouraged the horse forward and the entire procession moved towards the small farm worker's cottage which was the place which had been designated for the post-mortem to take place.

Bob brought the Clydesdale gently to a halt opposite the gate to the little yard and held her tight as the men lifted the coffin from the cart and with some difficulty carried it through the small cottage door and placed it on the kitchen floor. One of the Sextons then stepped forward and, using a heavy crowbar, prised open the lid of the coffin. All four men gasped and covered their faces with their jacket sleeves as the putrid smell invaded the little kitchen. With eyes averted, they lifted the body of Mary Jane out of the box and laid her gently on the table before, with some relief, heading back out into the fresh air. The doctors then closed the cottage door, leaving the sergeant and the vicar to wait in silence in the lane whilst they went about their unthinkable business.

An hour passed, then another, and those waiting in the lane shuffled their feet and huddled into their coats against the cold and the drizzling rain and tried to keep their minds away from what was taking place in the little building behind them. Eventually, the cottage door opened and the doctors emerged, signalling to the waiting men that they could go inside and replace the body into the coffin. The doctors then approached the waiting Sergeant and Dr Wardle reported in a hushed voice that it was their opinion that Mary Jane Dodds had been strangled with her own shawl, but that they had been unable to ascertain if the burns on her body had occurred before or after death. Sergeant Daley then thanked the doctors and gave instructions for the coffin to be placed on the cart, and the sad little procession then retraced their steps along the lane to the churchyard.

The crowd, still huddled together in the rain, were silent as the cart passed and the coffin was once again laid in the ground. Reverend Holliday read once again the prayers of committal. The sextons began to refill the grave and the sergeant left instructions that a guard should be posted in the churchyard to prevent any members of the press or curious sightseers from entering.

Meanwhile, in his cold, dank cell in Bishop Auckland, Matt waited. He had said little during his time there other than to give perfunctory answers to the sergeant's enquiries as to his name, age and place of residence. His calm exterior however belayed his inner torment, as images of what he imagined was taking place in Hamsterley flashed through his mind. He had lost all sense of time and reality, a cold numbness pervading every part of his being. He continued to sit perfectly still, staring straight ahead at the glazed green tiles of the cell wall, and that was how Sergeant Daley found him on his return to the Bishop Auckland Police Station. Asking Matt to stand, he informed him, without preamble, that following the results of that day's post-mortem, he was formally charging him with the wilful murder of his wife Mary Jane Dodds on the 20th of February 1908 within the house they shared in the village of Hamsterley in the County of Durham and that he would remain in custody until the following day, when he would appear before Bishop Auckland Magistrates.

Matt made no visible response to the sergeant's words; he continued to stare straight ahead of him, his eyes seemingly focused on some distant point beyond the confines of the cell. The sergeant had witnessed the reactions of many prisoners when faced with a serious charge; some became violent and had to be restrained, some fell to the ground and cried like babies, others screamed and shouted, but never in his twenty years in the force had he seen anyone react in such a calm, detached way as this man.

The two men remained facing each other in silence for a further few minutes before the officer turned to leave the cell. His movement seemed to awaken something in Matt and speaking in quiet voice he said: "I didn't dee it, that's all." As the Sergeant began to close the cell door Matt spoke again, requesting that someone should let his father know.

Chapter 7

The Bishop Auckland Magistrates Court was also in Bondgate, adjacent to the police station, and at ten o'clock the following morning Matt, flanked by two police officers, was led from his cell and through the heavy oak door which separated the two buildings. They walked in silence down a short, dark corridor at the end of which was a door which led directly into the courtroom.

Matt emerged into the presence of the town's three magistrates, who were seated behind a high oak bench. Glancing quickly around him, he saw that the public gallery was full of people, whilst coming from outside in Bondgate could be heard the clamour of hundreds more who were unable to gain entry. Matt's eyes scanned the faces in the gallery, but he failed to catch a glimpse of his father or his brother Charlie.

In a slow and sombre voice, the clerk of the court read the charge against Matt, following which he was requested to state his plea, to which he replied, "Not guilty". The existence of three wills and the benefits that his wife's death would bring for Matt formed the basis of the prosecution's case, along with the threats he had been heard to make against her life. Witnesses were called into the box, and after taking the oath, they gave one by one their accounts of the events of that fateful day in February and of what they had witnessed of the relationship between Matt and his late wife. The case for the defence rested simply on Matt's claim that was he was not in the house and did not kill his wife.

The clerk then called Dr George Wardle into the witness box to give the results of the post-mortem held on Mary Jane's body. Dr Wardle confidently stated that the examination carried out by his colleague Dr William Leigh and himself had revealed a straight line around the victim's neck and as a consequence they were in no doubt that death had been the result of strangulation. They had been unable to ascertain, however, whether the burning on the body had occurred before or after death. As he finished speaking there was a momentary silence before a collective intake of breath could be heard from those crowded into the gallery.

The magistrates thanked the witnesses before ceremoniously retiring to a small ante- chamber at the side of the courtroom. Within minutes they returned to their seats on the bench. Looking Matt directly in the eye, the senior magistrate informed him that they had reached a unanimous decision and that he would be taken to Durham Prison and there await trial at the next Quarter Session of the Assize Court for the murder of his wife Mary Jane Dodds.

Following this pronouncement, pandemonium broke out in the public gallery and fearing trouble, the three magistrates made a hasty and rather undignified exit from the court through the side door, while the two police officers roughly took hold of Matt's arms and hurriedly ushered him back through the door and into the safety of the police station. The whole procedure had taken less than ten minutes.

Back in his dismal little cell, Matt sat on the hard stone bench and desperately tried to gather his whirling thoughts and try and make sense of what had just happened. From outside he could still hear the hum of the excited crowd as the news of the verdict was passed from person to person. He had failed to see his father and brothers in the courtroom, and now he wondered if they were outside in the street being hassled by the crowd.

He could not rid his mind of thoughts of how reports of today's happenings would be received back in Hamsterley. Since the night of his arrest, he had had no contact with anyone from the village and had no knowledge of how his family was faring. Sitting in the cold, dank cell and putting his head into his hands, he prayed silently for his family in the hope that they were being supported by their friends and neighbours.

Matt had no means of knowing of the mounting hysteria which his case was generating, both in Hamsterley and throughout the county. The *Northern Echo* had carried a full account of the exhumation of Mary Jane's body, accompanied by grainy photographs which the paper's photographer had contrived to take at the time, despite the cordon of policemen. There were images of St James's and its little churchyard, the exhumed coffin being lifted onto Bob Thompson's hay cart, the coffin being carried into the little farm cottage where the gruesome event had taken place and of Matt's house, the scene of the alleged crime.

Stories were soon sweeping the neighbourhood with details of Matt and Mary Jane's troubled and often violent relationship. In village shops and public bars throughout the area people debated the significance of there being three wills and endlessly speculated over the horrifying revelation that a shawl had been tied around Mary Jane's neck.

Attitudes within Hamsterley were divided as a result of all this intense scrutiny and debate, proving Matt to be justified in his concern for his family. Close friends stood by them but the opinion of some of the villagers was hardening towards Matt.

Michael and Charlie were aware that there were those who were distancing themselves from the family. As they went about their business in the village, they were conscious of sideways glances and hushed conversations just out of their hearing. On the whole, though, there was a quiet sympathy for Michael Dodds, and in the little Baptist chapel prayers for the family were said each Sunday.

Opinion towards Mary Jane was changing too; there were an increasing number of customers in Mr Robson's shop who now spoke of Mary Jane as a tragic figure who had suffered greatly in her life. They recalled the deaths of her parents and the years of loneliness and shame she had endured following the suicide of her first husband. Many now claimed to have offered her sympathy and kindness when they had met her in the street and seen the cuts and bruises that were the evidence of the abuse and cruelty she had suffered at Matt's hands. They shook their heads and declared that the poor lass was to be pitied for the circumstances of her final years.

Chapter 8

The imposing prison in Durham City was built in 1810 and has six hundred cells, on three floors. It was built with money provided by Barrington Shute, the then Bishop of Durham, and stands on the site of several previous houses of correction dating back to the early fifteenth century. The building stands as one of the three main landmarks of the city, the others being the cathedral, which stands high on a peninsula on the River Wear and houses the shrine of St. Cuthbert, and the castle, built by the Normans as a bastion against the invading Scots. Although conditions inside the prison were much improved from its earlier days following the 1823 Prisons Act, life in Durham Prison was still harsh for its inmates.

Matt travelled the fifteen miles from Hamsterley to Durham in the back of a covered wagon handcuffed to two police officers, a cold and uncomfortable journey, the roads being muddy and deeply rutted. It was late evening by the time they arrived at the prison, where his name, age, height and physical features were recorded in the prison register by a surly warder who clearly resented Matt's arrival at the prison at such an hour.

Matt was then placed against the wall and instructed to place his hands up high against his chest whilst a second warder chalked his name and the date on a small slate which was above Matt's head. Satisfied that he was positioned correctly and with stern instructions that he was not to move, the warder then took a photograph for the prison records. Matt was then taken into a small side room where he was instructed to take off his clothes, which were placed in a bag to be held until such time as he appeared in court, and given a jacket and pair a of trousers both covered in black arrows, the standard prison uniform. Throughout all of this Matt remained calm and compliant, seeming to accept these humiliations without question.

Once everyone was satisfied that all the necessary paperwork was completed, Matt was then escorted, with a prison warder on each side, to his cell. He was pleased at least to find that although sparse, it was a big improvement on the cell in Bishop Auckland Police Station. The walls of this cell were covered with clean, glazed white tiles and there was a wooden bunk bed up against the far wall on which were placed a folded woollen blanket and a pillow with a striped cover. The only other item was in the corner, a metal bucket covered by a wooden lid. High in the wall above the bed was an eight-paned window, and although the hour was now late, it at least promised some daylight.

Matt adjusted to the daily life of the prison surprisingly quickly, appearing untroubled by the rigorous routine and the hours spent in solitude in his cell. It seemed that the experience in his childhood of being shunned by his peers and his subsequent tendency to be a loner had given him the mental strength needed to tolerate his incarceration.

As he was on remand and awaiting trial, in the eyes of the law he was not guilty of any crime and that entitled him to be treated in a different way from those convicted prisoners who were serving out their sentences. He enjoyed the relative luxury of a single cell in what was otherwise an overcrowded prison. His meals, served through the small hatch in the cell door, were of a slightly better quality than those dished out to the men in the main body of the prison and he was not required to spend hours each day in physical labour.

He was aware of the presence of other prisoners in the other parts of the jail, mainly through the sounds that echoed around the building. Each night he could feel the vibrations as the heavy iron cell doors slammed shut at lockdown and hear the clanging and rattling as the inmates emptied their buckets and bowls each morning. Quite often he would hear the sound of booted footsteps on the metal walkways as prisoners were moved around the building. Occasionally the cheerful sound of someone whistling a well-known tune would fill the air, or he would catch the words of a shouted greeting between inmates. There were times when the sounds within the prison were more ominous; the raised voices of a heated argument or the shouts of the prison warders and the shrill of whistles as they broke up a fight. One night he was awakened from his sleep by the sound of metal cups being banged against cell doors as the prisoners protested against some perceived injustice.

For the most part though, Matt's days passed unremarkably. Each morning he was awakened at six, and following his breakfast of porridge he was escorted by two warders to the prison yard for his daily exercise, half an hour walking its perimeter. This was the part of the day that lifted Matt's spirits, as it provided him with the welcome opportunity to see an open stretch of sky, no matter what the weather, and to hear the muffled songs of the city's birds.

Once a week he was paid a visit by the prison chaplain, a kindly man in his late sixties who, despite being familiar with the very worst of human nature, maintained a humble and generous disposition. Matt looked forward to these visits and the two of them spent a pleasant hour together with the chaplain encouraging him to speak about his family and life in Hamsterley. He appeared to be especially interested in Matt's Baptist background and his family's involvement with the historical little chapel in the village. On one visit the chaplain handed Matt a battered copy of the Bible, and he frequently brought him copies of printed religious pamphlets. The two always ended their time together in prayer, Matt seeming to draw the strength from their time together to endure the periods of confinement and loneliness.

Matt's letters written to family and friends indicated that he was keeping abreast of current and local affairs. He wrote three letters to John Heads, a friend who lived in Cockfield. In the first, written on March 3rd, he assured his friend that he was getting on fairly well and had plenty to eat and books and a daily newspaper to read. He was, he said, able to go to the chapel every day and take daily exercise. He also asked that if Mr Heads or anyone else were in Durham, they might visit him. In the second letter, dated 6th of June, he wrote of not having long to wait for the trial at the Assizes. He mentioned a shipyard strike and the distress it had caused in a lot of places, the Royal Show at Newcastle and the prospect of sports at Hamsterley on Whit Monday. His final letter to Mr Heads was dated the 18th of June and in it Matt spoke of his uncertainty as to the date of the trial and expressed his sadness at hearing of the death of his friend George Race, who, he remembered, used to give him a cup of hot tea when he was coming home from work on cold nights In Hamsterley.

However, there was little concern for the events taking place in the world beyond his own narrow boundaries. The newspapers that summer were full of lengthy reports recounting the successes of the athletes from Great Britain and Ireland at the Fourth Olympic Games being held in London that year. There was also extensive coverage of the activities of the Suffragettes and the increasing support around the country for their cause and of the ten-thousand-strong march through London to demand the vote for women.

Although these historic events were of fleeting interest to the inhabitants, the focus of Hamsterley's attention was centred on what the newspaper headlines were referring to as "The Hamsterley Tragedy" and all thoughts were on the impending trial.

Chapter 9

The date of the trial was set for the 29th of June and that morning dawned bright and sunny. At first light what seemed to be the entire adult population of Hamsterley were clamouring for seats on the train leaving Witton le Wear Station heading for Durham City. Everyone was wearing their Sunday best and many carried picnic baskets, and the atmosphere amongst the crowd was one of general excitement and a holiday spirit. With everyone packed liked sardines into the third-class carriages, the half-hour journey passed quickly as the train steamed through the grimy villages and past the tall pit winding wheels of the Durham coalfield.

Eventually the train slowed as it crossed over the hundred-foot-high viaduct at the approach to the city. From the height of the viaduct the villagers looked out over the jumble of rooftops, chimneys, ramshackle streets and backyards of the city, the whole scene being dominated by the mass of the cathedral and the castle.

Michael and Charlie Dodds were among the throng of people making their way out of the station and down the narrow cobbled streets into the marketplace. They paused briefly to take in the infamous statue of Charles William Vane Stewart, the Third Marquess of Londonderry, resplendent in his Hussar uniform and mounted on his horse. The statue had been erected in his memory by his wife, but was the object of much controversy and scorn amongst the miners of the county whom he was known to have exploited.

On a different occasion the two may have paused to inspect the intricate bronze which had been designed by the artist Raphael Monti and investigate the local legend of why the horse was missing its tongue. Today, however, they had no stomach for sightseeing and continued on their way, carried along by the momentum of the crowd, out of the marketplace and over the River Wear via Elvet Bridge towards the courthouse in Old Elvet.

Meanwhile, as the excited crowds were gathering around the city, Mr Justice Grantham stepped out of the door of the castle where he had spent a comfortable night, and into the waiting elaborate coach drawn by two magnificent horses. He set off on the short ride to the court, resplendent in his cape, stockings and shiny shoes, his head covered by a powdered white wig. The coach was driven by a liveried coachman wearing a three-cornered hat, and as was the tradition it was accompanied by four footmen dressed as in the eighteenth century. In front of the coach walked six policemen wearing helmets, three at the nearside holding long poles in their right hands and three at the offside carrying poles in their left hands. At the rear were a further two officers also carrying poles. The procession made its precarious way through the crowds and down the steep slope of Sadler Street, the horses slipping on the greasy cobbles. The coachman then negotiated the hazardous turn onto Elvet Bridge before drawing to a halt in front of the impressive stone-built courthouse.

Matt waited in his lonely cell unaware of all the excitement and ceremony in the city outside its walls. Each minute seemed like an hour as he stared at the door, his ears straining for the first sound of the heavy bolt on the other side being drawn back. At last two warders came. They placed him in handcuffs and solemnly escorted him out of the cell and along the corridor towards the musty, brick-lined tunnel that led from the prison to the courtroom.

Matt walked silently between the two men, breathing deeply in an attempt to calm his fears. Reaching the end of the tunnel and leaning heavily on his two sticks, he was helped up the tight wooden stairs into the dock and the full majesty of the courtroom, the combination of the steepness of the steps and his lameness causing him to breathe heavily from the effort. Steadying himself, he held onto the red railings bearing the ornate orb symbolising the monarch's power, and with the King's monogram picked out in gold.

In hushed voices, the onlookers in the public gallery commented to one another about his appearance. Although Matt appeared to be in a better state than when they had last seen him before the magistrates in Bishop Auckland, they noticed that he was thinner and that his face, though impassive, was ashen.

Looking directly ahead of him, Matt could see the legal men; for the prosecution, Messrs. Lowenthal and Mundahl, and for the defence, Mr E. Short and Mr S. Fleming, with their assistants on the benches behind them. Spread out on the green leather and gold inlay of their wooden desks in front of these learned gentlemen were their papers and documents.

To his left Matt noted the box containing the members of the jury, the men who would ultimately determine his fate and who now regarded him with expressionless faces. To his right, in a box propped up by mahogany pillars, were the representatives of the press, eager to note his every move and expression.

A movement on the crowded benches of the public gallery caught his eye and he smiled briefly as he recognised the familiar face of Mr Robson. Looking down from his elevated position above the court and seated in a huge red leather chair was the imposing figure of Mr Justice Grantham, a vast expanse of red leather covering the wooden desk in front of him and the royal coat of arms hanging powerfully above his wig like a crown.

The attention of the court was then drawn by the sound of the clerk and silence descended on the courtroom as he slowly read out the charge against Matt, who in reply stated "Not guilty" in a quiet, unwavering voice. Mr Lowenthal, dressed in his black silk gown, stiff white wing collar and horsehair wig, then took the floor and proceeded to outline the case for the prosecution. Standing before the jury, he informed them that at the time of her death Mary Jane Dodds had been in possession of several properties, having six or seven houses in the village of Hamsterley. They had to consider therefore to what extent the ownership of these properties had been an inducement to the prisoner to marry her in 1905. The couple had lived together unhappily throughout their short married life and it was without question that the prisoner ill-treated his wife from time to time and used threats against her such as "I'll strike your bloody brains out"; he had been heard to threaten her in this manner only a few days before her death. "It does not follow of course," he told them, "that he ever intended to carry out these threats, but you might have to take them into account when you are considering the case as a whole. There is no doubt though that the prisoner treated his wife with great cruelty."

Next he drew their attention to the matter of the evidence regarding certain wills which the deceased woman had made:

"In February 1907 in her first will, Mrs Dodds left all of her properties to her husband. Then on the twenty-second of August of last year, with the exception of £40 to her husband, along with certain other legacies, she left the whole of her property to her cousin Margaret Jane Pattison. Then on the 7th of January of this year, a man named William Henderson was asked to go to the house and witness another will. He was called into the house by the prisoner's brother. The prisoner and his wife were there and had a paper before them. Mr Henderson asked who had written out the will and the prisoner said he had copied it from the original will made out by Mr Holliday, the Vicar of Hamsterley. They, therefore, might like to consider whether Mrs Dodds was induced to make the third will – which left the whole of the property to the prisoner – in the hope that he would treat her better. The final will was the one which stood at the time of her death.

"It did not follow," Mr Lowenthal pointed out, "that because a man had a motive that he therefore committed a crime, but you must consider that the prisoner had lost all affection for his wife – if indeed he ever had any – that he knew she had previously altered her mind in regard to her will and property and that her husband knew on the 20th of February of this year that if she died without any further change of mind he stood to benefit in the extent of the whole property she possessed."

Mr Lowenthal then informed the jury that although Mary Jane was known to partake of drink, she was not considered to be a drunken woman. The evidence he put to them pointed strongly to the fact that on the 20th of February at any rate, she was not drunk. He was confident he would be able to establish that on the day in question the prisoner was in the house with his wife and the evidence would show that screaming was heard some time after two o'clock and that later there was no screaming. The inference was that the prisoner had strangled his wife and in order to conceal the crime had placed the body in the fender and set fire to it.

Mr Lowenthal stated: "From the position in which the body had been found, it is absolutely inconceivable, unless the woman had been quite unconscious or helplessly drunk, that she could have allowed herself to remain in that position, near the fender, whilst her clothing was on fire". He reminded them that the policeman was not at the house until five o'clock and that he had stated that when he arrived the body was in such a state that stiffness appeared to be setting in. There was no fire in the grate, but there were large cinders on the hearth and the fire looked as though it had been raked out.

He reminded them also that Dr Cunliffe had arrived at about 7.30 and that there was not much light then for examination. The doctor had formed the opinion that death was not through shock – which would be the cause of death in such a case as this if death took place from burns – but he did not form any opinion then as to what the cause of death in fact was, not having made a proper examination.

"Up to that time there was no idea – except in the mind of Dr Cunliffe – that death was not occasioned by burns," he told them. He said that no medical evidence had been called at the inquest, and the verdict of the Coroner was that the deceased had apparently died from burns, but there was no evidence to show how the burns were received. After the inquest the deceased woman was buried, but subsequently, after the body had been in the grave for 16 days, there was an exhumation and post-mortem examination. The evidence forthcoming following the exhumation and post-mortem was conclusive as to what had caused this woman's death: there was a definite line encircling her neck and there was swelling and a marked blue colour above the line, whilst below there was the normal white skin."

If the jury was satisfied that death resulted from strangulation, he told them, then there still remained the question as to who did it. If it was caused by another person then, he supposed, they would not be able to entertain the slightest doubt that the prisoner caused it. If, however, their minds were really satisfied that the prisoner did commit this dreadful crime, then in the interests of justice and the general public, he asked them to return a verdict of guilty.

Mr Lowenthal then called witnesses to the box from the benches arranged along the side wall of the court. An architect by the name of Mr F H Livesay gave evidence regarding the situation of the prisoner's house at Hamsterley and the position and distances of other property. He also gave details of the measurements of the fire-grate and the fender in the room in which the body of the deceased was found lying.

Several villagers were then called to give their accounts of the events of that fatal day. George Wilfred Marr, Reverend Holliday and Sarah Wade, who had previously given evidence at the inquest, were called again. Then James Jopling Brown, a medical student living at Hamsterley, took the stand and stated that on the day in question he was travelling in a trap to Witton Park and as he passed Mrs Dodds' house at about two thirty-five he had heard screaming, which continued until he drove out of hearing. After the funeral of the deceased on the 23rd of February, he had gone to the prisoner's house with a will which his brother who was an articled clerk to a solicitor had drawn up. He confirmed that at that point the prisoner had produced a later will. James said that he had read both the wills but that he thought the third will was the one which would stand.

A very nervous Jane Braithwaite, who was employed at the Cross Keys, was then called. In a quiet voice she told the court that on the day in question she had supplied Mrs Dodds with a gill of beer and later at about two o'clock, a shilling's worth of whisky. When asked by Mr Lowenthal, she said that she heard screams coming from Mrs Dodds' house. She confirmed that she had twice seen Mrs Dodds with black eyes and that on one occasion the deceased had shown her the black and blue marks on her arm. Asked if she had ever seen the deceased drunk, Jane replied that she had not, although Mrs Dodds was in the habit of getting beer two or three times a day.

Alice Stephenson then took the stand and confirmed that her husband was the landlord of the Cross Keys. On the day in question Mrs Dodds had visited the pub at about half past eight in the morning and got a gill of beer. At about twenty to two on the same day she purchased a shilling's worth of whisky and seemed to be sober.

"Would you call Mrs Dodds a drunken woman?" Mr Lowenthal asked her.

"No, I would not," she replied, "I would say that she was a woman who took drink."

Alice also stated that she had on one occasion seen the prisoner kick his wife and she had also known times when Mrs Dodds knocked on her own door during the night and asked her husband to let her into the house.

Garthwaite Wilkinson, a young man from the village, confirmed that he had been emptying ashpits when he saw Mrs Dodds at about, he thought, a quarter to two, and she had given him a glass of whisky which he drank. He had later seen the prisoner leave the house and proceed to the joiner's shop. He thought it would be about twenty to three when the prisoner left the house, and he had heard no shouting at all. After this, whilst he was out with his cart, the prisoner had ridden in his cart from the joiner's shop to the blacksmith's shop.

Mr Lowenthal then called Elizabeth Ann Marquis, but there was some difficulty in obtaining her evidence as she was extremely deaf. She told the court that early in the afternoon of the day in question Mrs Dodds was quite sober when she had come to her house for coal and sticks. Mr Marquis had later noticed the prisoner go into the archway leading to his house. Shortly afterwards she saw someone pull the blind down in the sitting room. Later, about four o'clock, she saw someone whom she believed to be the prisoner pull it up again. Then, a few minutes later, she saw the prisoner come from the archway, go to Robson's shop and afterwards to his father's house, returning to his own house with his father's housekeeper. It was not long, she said, before the prisoner came out of his house again. She then confirmed that she had often been in Mrs Dodds' house but had never seen her sitting on the sitting-room fender. She had often seen Mrs Dodds with black eyes and black marks, and on one occasion she had seen her master, Mr Watson, examine Mrs Dodds' neck.

The previous witness's evidence was confirmed by Joseph Watson, a farm labourer, who said that the deceased was in his house about one-thirty on the day in question and was perfectly sober. When he went out she had remained in the house. He also confirmed that in December she had complained to him and he had examined her neck, which was swollen.

William Race, a coke drawer, confirmed that on the 20th of February he was in the blacksmith's shop at Hamsterley when the prisoner came in at about three-fifteen and remained about fifteen minutes, and that he had talked to him.

Mary Hannah Blackett told Mr Lowenthal she had often seen the deceased with bruises and cuts on her head and that Mrs Dodds had several times complained to her. She was asked to recall the incident when she had found Mrs Dodds lying on the floor in her house. She also said that she had heard the prisoner use threatening language to his wife on another occasion when she had seen him put her out of the door. He had a sweeping brush in his hand and had struck her and said: "I'll kill you" before putting her in the wash-house. She had been all right for drink that time, Mrs Blackett said, but on certain occasions she had seen her the worse for drink.

The evidence of Dorothy Hodgson was then read out to the court. She was formerly housekeeper for the prisoner's father, Michael John Dodds, but he had since died. The evidence read that as far as Mrs Hodgson could remember, the prisoner came to his father's house on the day in question about four o'clock and said that his wife had been burnt to death.

When Mr Short cross-examined these witnesses, there was much discussion around the discrepancies in their accounts of the timing of events, the number of voices that had been heard coming from the inside the house, the matter of the wills and the position in which Mary Jane's body had been found. Mr Short suggested to James Brown that he had altered his evidence with regard to times after speaking with the Reverend Holliday, and Mr Brown denied this. He also pressed Alice Stephenson about the kicking incident and ascertained that she had not contacted the police or attempted to help Mrs Dodds.

Mr Short challenged Reverend Holliday over his statement at the inquest that he had seen the prisoner leave his house at two-thirty but had now changed his evidence, saying it was about two-forty-five or two-fifty. Mr Holliday denied that he had fixed the time after discussing the issue with James Brown.

Sarah Wade was then recalled, and Mr Short asked her if she had ever heard Mrs Dodds say unkind things to her husband. Sarah confirmed that she had. When asked if she taunted him about his deformity, Sarah replied, "Yes". The Judge then asked her which fire was usually lit in the Dodds' house. She said that from three weeks before Christmas, the sitting-room fire was always lit. The kitchen fire was not lit because there were two large window panes out in the kitchen.

Once Mr Short had ended his questioning, as the hour was growing late, Mr Justice Grantham adjourned the court until ten o'clock the following day. Matt was then led back down the narrow steps and through the dingy tunnel to his cell for the night.

Chapter 10

Proceedings began again promptly at ten the next morning with the evidence of PC Lowe, who described events after he was called to the prisoner's house. He described how the prisoner had told him that he had found his wife's body in the same position as it was now with her back to the fire, adding that he had pulled her out of the fireplace by the arm. The prisoner had told him that his wife had some drink in the house and that she had given him a glass of whisky and also given a glass to Garthwaite Wilkinson, and that he had thrown another glassful into the fire. The prisoner had stated that his wife was drunk.

At this point the fender was brought into the courtroom and the exact position of the body indicated. P C Lowe described the deceased's face as being a dark bluish colour, whilst the lips were swollen. He did not, he added, see the throat. The body was very much burnt back and front, and the clothing was burnt off except some of the shoulders and the bottom of the skirt. There was no fire in the grate but there were a few cinders, and some cinders were strewn on the fender, appearing to have been raked out of the fireplace. He had then left the house with the prisoner and he had locked the door.

Returning with Doctor Cunliffe, he noticed this time that the deceased's mouth was open. He described how the doctor had found a poker beneath the body and a cinder clasped in her hand. When he left the house with the doctor he had again locked the door. He had then cycled to West Auckland to see Sergeant Martin, arriving at ten o'clock. The Sergeant returned with him to the prisoner's house the same night, when he went across to Michael Dodd's house and woke the prisoner up to go with them. When asked if at any time he had noticed any marks of burning on the hearthrug, the constable replied that there were not. He then confirmed that neither he nor Dr Cunliffe were called at the inquest.

Proceeding, PC Lowe described the incident at the end of the previous year when he had been called after midnight to the disturbance at the prisoner's house.

George Thomas Spence, undertaker, of Hamsterley, gave evidence that the prisoner had called upon him on the evening of the 20th of February and ordered a coffin to be made for his wife, who had been found burnt to death. He had returned with the prisoner to the house and found the deceased on the hearth rug and covered with a sheet. At this time he was not able to take measurements as the body was in a crouched position. He had returned the next morning for this purpose after the body had been prepared. He had, he said, noticed that the deceased's face was swollen and a dark colour.

The next person into the witness box was

Mary Liddle, who said that on the morning after the woman's death she was called to attend to the body. She noticed blood on the carpet, which appeared to have flowed from the mouth. The face was blue-black and the neck, face and lips were much swollen. She then described how she had found the burnt shawl tied round the neck, but she did not notice how it was tied. She told how Mrs Knaggs, who was with her, had assisted in cutting it off.

She then told of how on the 10th of March she saw the coffin after it was taken out of the grave and removed to a cottage where doctors were in attendance. She identified the body on this occasion. When the coffin was opened she noticed the face, which did not appear quite so swollen as on the 21st of February. Answering the Judge, she said the body was very black and much burnt.

Mary Knaggs corroborated the previous witness's evidence, saying the neck, lips and mouth were much swollen. She had looked among the cinders on the fender and found steels from the deceased's corset; a small part of the corset remained attached to the steel. She had found the steel at the opposite end of the fender to where the deceased's head was found lying.

At this point the remains of Mary Jane's clothing were brought into the courtroom by the police and Mr Justice Grantham carefully examined a portion of them. John Thomas Proud, the Coroner, then confirmed that he had held an inquest at Hamsterley on the body of Mary Jane Dodds and that the prisoner had been sworn in and had given evidence. Mr Justice Grantham asked if the prisoner gave the story himself or if the story was in answer to questions. Mr Proud explained that it was his practice to ask questions. Mr Lowenthal then read out Matt Dodds' statement from the inquest that he had found his wife burnt to death in the house at about four o'clock on the day in question. Mr Proud then confirmed that the prisoner had not been able to account for the witnesses' claims of hearing shouting.

Mr Short then asked the Coroner about the times stated by the witnesses and the Reverend

Holliday, and Mr Proud said he could not recollect all the details exactly. Mr Justice Grantham asked why a doctor was not called at the inquest, to which Mr Proud replied that at the time the case was thought to be one of burning. Mr Proud confirmed that he thought the case was not free from suspicion, and agreed that in the light of what had since taken place it would have been very much better if there had been a post-mortem. He added: "If I had known what I knew three days later I would have adopted that course. As it was, an open verdict was returned and I instructed the police to make further investigation".

"You did instruct the police?" asked the Judge.

"Oh yes, and after their inquiries I at once communicated with the Home Office."

The Judge expressed satisfaction with the course which had been taken and further asked: "You had not before you the evidence of the two women who had laid out the body?" The Coroner replied: "No, My Lord, nor did we know anything about it."

Returning to the matter of the wills, John Edward Brown, solicitor's clerk, spoke of the drawing up of a will for the deceased, and William Henderson confirmed that he had witnessed it and that Mrs Dodds was quite willing to sign it. He had, he said, known the deceased for many years and had never known her drunk.

The different wills were then read to the jury by Mr Mundahl. Mary Jane Pattison of Bishop Auckland was then called, and she explained how she had proceeded to the prisoner's house after the funeral and had subsequently heard two wills read by Mr Brown. She confirmed that she knew of the will in Mr Brown's charge because her cousin had told her it was there in case anything happened to her. She had been on very friendly terms with the deceased and said she had not told her anything about a fresh will.

In answer to Mr Short's questions, she said that she knew her cousin took a little drink and that the couple quarrelled a good deal. She thought that in their quarrels one was as bad as the other. Whenever she visited the house, the prisoner was very kind to his wife, but she heard they quarrelled in her absence.

Sergeant Martin from West Auckland next spoke of his visit to the house on the night of the 20th of February. He had seen no signs of a struggle and noticed that the hearthrug was not burnt. When he had asked the prisoner as to when he had last seen his wife, he had replied: "I saw her at half-past two sitting on a chair between the fireplace and the window, drunk." Asking the prisoner when he found his wife in this state he had replied: "I came over from the workshop about four o'clock and found her lying dead between the grate and the fender. I went for Mrs Wade." Sergeant Martin then said that in regard to the bolt on the side door of the house he got PC Gould to shut the bolt whilst he went into Robson's shop to listen. He could hear the bolt shut quite plainly.

The remainder of the morning was given over to the medical evidence. Dr George Wardle entered the witness box next, to give an account of the post-mortem which he, assisted by Dr

Cunliffe, had carried out on the exhumed body, whilst Dr Leigh took notes. He added that Dr Farquharson was also present on behalf of the prisoner. The doctor described the burns on the body and said that the trunk was severely burned to the consistency of burnt leather. The left hand was clenched and the thumb in the palm, but the right hand was limp. The face and neck were much swollen and congested as low down as a well- defined line level with what was commonly called the Adam's apple. This line, limiting the swollen conditions, extended round the neck. Above the line, the colour was dark and below the line there was not swelling or congestion and the colour was the usual livid colour of a corpse.

In answer to a question from the Judge, Doctor Wardle confirmed that this line was what he would expect to find from anything put tightly round the neck. Continuing, the doctor described how the muscles on the sides of the neck were swollen, as was the neck generally. As to the internal examination, Doctor Wardle reported that there were no signs of injury to the trachea.

On removal of the scalp, he found the vessels highly engorged, as were the superficial vessels of the brain. This, he explained, indicated that the circulation of blood in these structures had been arrested at the lower level. He had also found present certain minute red points indicating that there had been a congested state of the small blood vessels in the brain. When asked by Mr Lowenthal if he was able to form an opinion as to what had caused this woman's death, Doctor Wardle stated that it was his considered opinion that death had been caused by strangulation brought about by means of a constricting band and that this strangulation had resulted in suffocation or asphyxia indentation.

Mr Short intervened at this point and the witness confirmed in answer to his questions that the body had shown no signs or marks of violence and that there had been no froth in the windpipe. Mr Lowenthal then asked: "Have you any doubt whatever that the death was caused by strangulation by the band round the neck?" to which Dr Wardle replied: "I have no doubt whatever, I can think of no other explanation".

Mr Justice Grantham asked: "Assuming she had fallen from the chair into the fire, can you imagine or understand how the trunk of the body should have been burnt all round in an even manner?" Doctor Wardle replied: "I don't see how it could happen that way. I don't see how she could fall on the fire from the description I have heard of the grate."

Doctor Cunliffe of Witton Park was then called and he recalled how he was called to the prisoner's house and arrived there about 7.30 on the evening of the 29th of February accompanied by PC Lowe. He described the position of the body, agreeing with what had been stated by other witnesses. The eyes, he said, were partly open and prominent and he noticed a cinder clenched in the left hand. The hand, he added, was difficult to open. The body was markedly stiff and he thought she had been lying dead for four or five hours. It was dark when he made the visit and his examination was by the light of a candle held by the policeman. He formed an opinion that the woman had not died from burning, but did not form an opinion as to the actual cause of death. He had been present at the post-mortem, after the exhumation, and he agreed with the evidence of Dr Wardle. He concluded that the woman had died from strangulation.

When asked by Mr Short, he could not remember if Dr Farquharson had requested that the scalp should be shaved, nor did he remember him calling attention to an abrasion, but he thought he had mentioned a small eruption on the scalp.

"Do you admit that Dr Farquharson drew attention to something on the scalp?" Mr Short persisted.

"Yes, he called it eczema and I called it an eruption. I think it was due to singeing of the hair."

Dr Leigh of Bishop Auckland confirmed that he had taken notes at the post-mortem examination and made observations. The sharp line of demarcation round the neck led him to conclude that death was the result of asphyxia due to some constricting band having been placed around it.

Mr Stock, the County Analyst, then gave evidence as to the analysis of the contents of the stomach and other organs of the deceased. In the stomach there had been found 2.32 ounces of absolute alcohol, which he explained was equivalent to a tablespoon and a half of whisky. He had tested the blood for carbon monoxide and discovered no evidence of its presence. A microscope examination of a piece of skin did not result in the finding of any abrasion. Cross-examined by Mr Fleming, he said that what alcohol he had found gave no evidence of the amount which had been absorbed.

The next person to enter the witness box was Dr Pepper of London, who was introduced to the court as the Consultative Adviser to the Home Office. After confirming that he had very wide experience of post-mortem examinations, having conducted almost five thousand himself, Dr Pepper said he had heard the evidence given previously and read the depositions and that he was able to form a clear idea of what had been the cause of Mrs Dodds' death.

"What in your opinion caused her death?" he was asked by Mr Lowenthal.

"Obstruction of the circulation by compression of the neck."

"Have you been able to form an opinion as to how the obstruction was produced?" Mr Lowenthal continued.

"Clearly by some soft, resisting body applied round the neck."

Dr Pepper explained that he had come to this conclusion owing to extreme discolouration above a well-defined line and normal conditions below. This, he said, was consistent only with pressure from a band round the neck. He thought the band in this case had been soft, because if it had been hard there would have been not only demarcation but an actual mark in the skin. Unless drawn unnecessarily tight, the shawl would not have caused abrasion of the skin or indentation. With a degree of swelling showing, he should say death might take place in half a minute. It might be longer or less. There was no material difference between blisters produced before death and blisters produced quite immediately after death. Nothing could account for the conditions above and below the mark round the neck but the application of a constricting band.

When the Judge enquired if it was possible that the band might have been tightened accidentally, he explained that a person might become unconscious and become in such a condition that whatever was round the neck gripped it, but he would not expect this to occur in a body lying in a horizontal position.

Mr Short then asked the witness about the grasping of the cinder by the deceased, and he thought this would not indicate any struggle. It was probable that she clutched it in her death struggle, which would indicate that she was inside the fender at the time of death. Some swelling might arise by the woman's head hanging over the fender.

This concluding the case for the prosecution, Mr Lowenthal returned to his place and Mr Justice Grantham adjourned the court for lunch.

Chapter 11

On the resumption of the proceedings, Mr Short took to the floor for the case for the defence and spoke powerfully and at length. He began by telling the jury that he was not quite sure whether the case for the prosecution was that the prisoner first strangled his wife and then put her on the fire or whether, as shown by Dr Pepper, she was in fact living when she was put on the fire. His hope, he told them, was to be able to satisfy them that there was not sufficient evidence to justify them saying that the prisoner did whatever was done. It was not his duty, he told them, to give explanations or start theories as to how this woman came by her death; that was for the prosecution, who had to satisfy the jury of the prisoner's guilt. It was not he who had to satisfy them of the prisoner's innocence.

It had been claimed that the prisoner had a motive, to deprive the woman of her life before she had the opportunity to alter her will again. The prosecution's claim therefore pointed to this being a deliberately planned murder for the purpose of gaining possession of the money, but he put it to them that all the probabilities of the case were absolutely against that theory. It might be true that the prisoner had previously used threats and some violence against his wife, but the threats had not been carried out.

Unfortunately, there had been some amount of drinking by this woman and he did not think they could have any doubt that these drinking habits led to their quarrelling. However, there had been no suggestion whatsoever that the prisoner himself was drunk on any of these occasions.

One thing was quite clear: that in regard to the third will, the woman herself took a prominent part in having it executed and witnessed, and it was she who suggested to William Henderson, the blacksmith, that he should not say anything about it to anyone. The only possible evidence that the prisoner induced her to make the will was that he copied it out in his own handwriting.

Could they find anything in the prisoner's past conduct pointing to deliberate intention to kill? If he had made up his mind in this direction, would he not have taken care to have appeared more kindly towards her? Did they suppose that having got the will and intending to kill the woman, he would have allowed to give himself away by threatening her and showing violence within a short time of her death? It was inconsistent with the suggestion of the motive set up by the prosecution.

Did they believe the prisoner was a sufficiently accomplished actor to have committed the awful crime, gone about perfectly calmly, and then when the time came to tell other people about it that he could have pretended all his distress and shock? The whole of his conduct was inconsistent with his knowing anything about how this woman came by her death. He had answered every question openly and frankly and from the first moment he had mentioned it to anyone, from the first moment he was questioned, his story had been quite consistent as to how he had last seen her and how he had found her. Everything about his conduct pointed to his innocence and nothing to his guilt.

If he could establish a reasonable doubt as to whether the prisoner was in the house at the time, Mr Short continued, he was convinced the jury would have difficulty in finding a verdict other than not guilty. At best, the evidence as to minutes and moments was difficult and unreliable. Would it be fair to take the evidence of Mr Holliday as reliable? Was his evidence sufficiently reliable to justify them acting upon it? At the inquest, Mr Holliday stated that it would be 2.35 when he saw the prisoner leaving the house. At that time, he had forgotten about looking at the clock and so on and had forgotten all about what he now told them he remembered. He believed they did it for the best, but Mr Brown did discuss the question of the time with Mr Holliday. Could they really rely on this evidence?

He ventured to suggest that there was no really reliable evidence as to time. They must look at the question from a broader standpoint than that of minutes and seconds. He thought he would show that the prisoner could not have been in the house when the shouting was going on. Was it conceivable that young Wilkinson could have been so near and not heard the shouting? Wilkinson stated that the prisoner had left before he left. Could they, in face of this, say the prisoner was in the house when the screaming took place?

Another point was that the witnesses who spoke of the shouting said they had only heard the deceased woman's voice, whilst on previous occasions they had heard two voices. Of the witnesses Waistell, Braithwaite and the medical student Brown, not one of them thought the shouting was to call for their assistance. If the prisoner was trying to kill and there had been all this shouting, would there not have been more evidence of struggle – some mark of violence? They knew the deceased was wearing the shawl at one o'clock because Mrs Wade saw her. The prisoner was a cripple and it would be extremely difficult for him to seize the woman and render her senseless without some act of violence on his part. There was no suggestion that he had stunned her and then strangled her. If they had any reasonable doubt raised in their minds, they would not allow the doctors' evidence to make it more conclusive. The doctors could only give opinions and nothing more. The fact of the cinder being clenched in the woman's hand shows she was alive at any rate for some period when she got onto the fender. If this lame man was taking her to the fire to put her on, he would have been bound to use considerable force, and if he had used it there would have been some indication of violence.

Continuing, Mr Short said it was noteworthy

that on the day in question the deceased had borrowed coals and sticks and these had not been used. There was evidence that she had commenced drinking early in the day and got whisky about the middle of the day. If she had not been going out in the afternoon, it was quite possible that she might rake out the fire in order to save consumption of the fuel. If anything occurred which caused her to fall on her left side with her back to the grate, she might catch fire in the way described.

He went on to say that however reluctant people might have been to say anything derogatory about this woman's character, they had facts which pointed strongly to her condition that day and there was evidence that she had access to drink other than that which she had bought at the Cross Keys on that particular day. It was admitted that she was in the habit of sitting on the kitchen fender and generally sat there when under the influence of drink. If she had sat down on the sitting room fender, thinking it was the kitchen fender, she would fall in just the way any person would fall under those circumstances. Her head would probably catch the grate. She would clutch at anything and being stunned, she might fall over the fender just in the position in which she might become insensible very quickly. Before the shawl was burnt it might be caught by her arm and become tightened. His theory was that she was doing something at the fireplace when she fell and was found in the manner described.

As to the shutting of the bolt of the door, did they think that if the prisoner wanted to prevent people coming in he would have shut the door in a way that could be heard? There was not much dispute as to the medical evidence except in regard to the evidence of a blow – not a severe blow – on the back of the deceased's head. there would be difference of opinion as to the conclusions of the doctors, but he would ask them not to decide the case on opinions.

Matt Dodds was then called, and he made his way slowly and rather awkwardly on his sticks to the witness box, seeming to stumble as he made his way up the short flight of steps. Despite this he looked calm and sanguine, keeping his eyes focused on Mr Fleming, who questioned him. He confirmed that he worked at the Seven Sisters Colliery at Cockfield as well as helping out in his father's joinery workshop. This was, he said, the first trouble he had ever been in. He was 44 years of age and had known his late wife all his life and had married her in 1905, but their life had not been altogether happy. He admitted that he had sometimes used threats against his wife, though he had had no intention of hurting her. When asked about the lost teeth, cut lips etc. spoken of by witnesses, Matt said she had fallen off the ashpit wall. She told him she had climbed up to gather eggs, because the hens used to go on the manure heap. He had been at work and she was in bed when he returned. When asked about his wife being seen with a black eye last Christmas, he explained that she had got this by falling against the step of a trap. He had been in his house when this took place and his wife told him about it.

Regarding the incident of kicking his wife, mentioned by Mrs Stephenson, he stated: "As a matter of fact, my wife was attacking me and I shoved her away. My wife was in the habit of calling me awful names and the quarrels we had were altogether about her drinking habits. As to her being found out at nights, when she used to be drinking, she was in the habit of going out. I had to be up at quarter to five in the morning and so I went to bed early. When I was awakened by her knocking I got up and let her in."

When questioned about the 20th of February, he said: "I did not myself hear any screaming on that day. There was no truth in the suggestion that any time during that afternoon I was in the house doing injury to my wife. There's no truth in it at all." He added that the story he had told the Coroner and the police was quite true. He also denied having said that his wife gave him whisky on that day and he did not know Wilkinson had had any until the next day.

Mr Lowenthal then stood up to question him, and in reply he stated that it was not true that his wife had continually had black eyes and that he had not given her any. He admitted, however, that he had struck her, but he denied ever having knocked her to the ground. He had heard Mrs Wade say she had seen him strike her and knock her down, but that was not true. He did not remember the incident referred to by the witness Mary Blackett and it was not correct that he had knocked his wife down. He had never got hold of her by the neck. On the occasion referred to by the policeman, he had heard her tell the constable that she did not want to live with him. When asked about the wills, Matt confirmed that he knew of the second will a week or two after it was made.

Returning to the events of the 20th of February, he said that his wife was not drunk at dinner time on that day, but she was under the influence of drink. He agreed that he was in the house at half past two in the afternoon, but said he had just come in from the workshop for a minute to get a spokeshave. He was adamant that he had not been in again until four. When asked about the blind, he said that it was up on both occasions and he did not put it up or down.

He was then asked about Mr Holliday and said he had not seen the vicar that day until night. “The suggestion that I was in the house from half past two until about ten minutes to three is quite untrue. When I returned to the house at four o’clock, my wife was lying burnt within the fender.”

At the conclusion of Matt’s evidence, the Judge adjourned the court until the next morning.

Chapter 12

The third day's proceedings began with the hearing of medical evidence for the defence. Dr A.C. Farquharson from Bishop Auckland took the stand and said he had performed upwards of seven hundred post-mortems to date in the course of his career. He had attended the post-mortem after the exhumation. Where the singeing was on the back of the head, he observed a slight abrasion or breaking of the surface of the skin. It was not an abrasion likely to have been caused by a heavy blow. He had attached importance to it at the time and drawn attention to it. On the interior – within the scalp – he saw indications corroborating what he had seen on the outside. The condition of the *dura mater* was such as to cause suspicion of a diseased brain – more than suspicion. He suggested that a portion should be examined microscopically, but this had not been done. If the brain was diseased, the slight blow which had caused the abrasion would cause insensibility.

Mr Short then asked him as to the theory set up by the prosecution. Assuming that the constricting band - the shawl – was drawn tight enough to cause death in half a minute, he would have expected to find indentation. If death was caused by a constricting band, he would have expected to find the eyes and tongue protruding and also to find froth. These were not present at the post-mortem. He would also have expected to find, under the skin around the neck, blood or fluid. Two incisions were made at the sides of the neck and under one side no fluid was found, whilst on the other side there were only a few drops. He would have expected to find a disturbance about the windpipe, and in the larynx some froth. The indications he saw negated the idea of rapid strangulation. The symptoms were not of death in half a minute. In his opinion death would take from ten to fifteen minutes.

He had heard the prisoner's story of finding his wife with her head hanging over the fender. If she had been lying in that position, insensible, that would be consistent with her dying by slow strangulation. In a protracted death he would have expected to find the internal organs normal, as they were in fact found to be.

Cross-examined by Mr Lowenthal, the doctor said the appearance of the deceased's face suggested some constricting influence. He could not account for the blueish colour above the line encircling the neck and the normal state below the line otherwise than by some constricting influence. Mr Lowenthal then quoted from a work by Professor Mann to the effect that protrusion of the tongue occurred in under fifty per cent of cases of strangulation.

Further replying to Mr Lowenthal, Dr Farquharson said the state of the brain did not suggest extreme obstruction to the circulation. He suspected disease of the brain, considerably advanced, from what he saw. Mr Short then quoted from another work on strangulation and the probable appearances.

This concluded the evidence, and Mr Short addressed the jury. He asked: "What can we decide when doctors disagree?" In summing up, he reminded the members of the jury that the theory of the prosecution was what they had to face, and unless they could accept it as absolutely proved, even if his own theory was the biggest load of rubbish in the world, the case for the prosecution must fail. Were they satisfied that there was nothing found inconsistent with rapid strangulation? That she died from strangulation, wholly or in part, there could be no doubt, but the question was, did the prisoner tie that shawl so as to strangle the deceased? If they were not satisfied that the prisoner did it, they would not be justified in finding him guilty. If there was any doubt about the matter being conclusive, then they could not convict. It was not for the prisoner to explain but for the prosecution to show that the prisoner was there and did what was suggested had been done. Could they, after the evidence of Littlefair and Wilkinson – which was not tainted with the suspicion that it might be wrong because it dealt with minutes and seconds – could they decide that it was conclusive that the prisoner was in the house at the time suggested by the prosecution? The prisoner might have denied, in the box, more than he ought to have denied, but they must remember his awful position. There must be some allowance for this wretched man.

"If this crime is proved," he continued, "it is not only a murder but a very bad murder. If the theory of the prosecution is correct, it is a cruel and bad murder and just one of those cases, which, if your verdict is guilty, no recommendation for mercy can be possibly have any effect. I don't, for one instant, ask you to shirk your duty or responsibility, but I ask you to remember that for all practical purposes it is in your hands that the life of the prisoner lies". Pausing briefly to look each juryman in the eye, he then continued

"Can you say, that upon the evidence, you could conclude definitely as to this man's guilt? Can you come to a conclusion which would justify you in sending a fellow creature to a felon's death?"

As Mr Short regained his seat, Mr Lowenthal stood up again. "So far as the theory of the prosecution is concerned, the only theory is that the prisoner did, beyond a possibility of doubt, strangle this woman." On hearing this, Matt was seen to shake his head. "My duty," continued Mr Lowenthal, "is to bring before you all the facts for and against and leave to the jury the determination of the question. I should be shirking my duty and be afraid of it if I were to allow myself to suggest that upon the evidence you can have the slightest doubt about the prisoner's guilt."

If the jury thought the prisoner was not at home at the time, he continued, they would acquit him. But, he thought, he would be able to establish it independently of time. They were asked to believe a whole series of amazing assumptions. As to Mr Holliday's evidence, he could not imagine any more serious responsibility and could not imagine any man more likely to appreciate the tremendous responsibility than a man like Mr Holliday, vicar of the parish. It was true he made a mistake as to the time at the inquest and instead of sticking to the mistake his duty compelled him to tell the truth after he had more completely recalled his movements on the day in question. He asked the jury to accept Mr Holliday's evidence as absolutely true. Independent of the evidence as to time, however, he thought he was able to establish the case against the prisoner.

"I think," he continued, "it is proved beyond all possibility of doubt that he was in the house and that it is proved this woman died from strangulation." There was no disagreement between the doctors on the only material question. He added, "I cannot submit you can rightly discharge your duty except by finding this man guilty."

The cases of both the prosecution and the defence being concluded, Mr justice Grantham summed up at great length, remarking at the outset that it was a serious case and the responsibility was great to everyone engaged in it. Yet, if the jury had no doubt that the effect of the evidence was that the prisoner charged was the person, if they had no doubt that death was at the hands of the prisoner charged, however unpleasant it might be for them, they had a duty to perform to society and must give effect to that view by their verdict. He thought now, after the evidence given by the prisoner, and more particularly after the speech on his behalf, there could be no doubt that death was due to strangulation and that the statement made by the prisoner that she died from burning was untrue. It might be that the prisoner was mistaken and it must be assumed that because of the false story the prisoner necessarily strangled her. But it had considerable bearing on the case and must have some bearing on the verdict. There was no suggestion that strangulation was suicidal, but it was suggested by the prisoner that it was accidental. If not accidental, by whom was it done? There was no suggestion it was by anyone else but the prisoner. If intentional, it was by the prisoner.

"If you come to the conclusion," his lordship continued, "that death resulted from strangulation and that she was strangled by somebody, then I am sorry to say there is no doubt the person must have been the prisoner." Motives were really a secondary consideration and if a motive was found they ought not to rely too much upon it. They ought not to assume that because there was a motive, therefore the prisoner committed the murder. The circumstances of the motive were remarkable. He thought there could be no doubt this couple lived a very unhappy life and no doubt – although it was for the jury to find and not him – that the prisoner was cruel and unkind. That being the relationship, it was not to be wondered at that in the summer of last year the woman should alter her will. He could quite understand her not wanting to go to the vicar again about the will – she would not want him to know. She went to a person who knew something about these matters. The single thing about the last will was that it was not drawn up by the clergyman or solicitor's clerk but the prisoner got hold of the original document and copied it for himself – about the worst thing a man could do. If it was honest, why did he not go to the solicitor's clerk? The deceased had told her cousin where the proper will was if anything happened to her.

It was very unfortunate for the prisoner that such was his conduct, because the fact could not be disguised that he had a motive that his wife should die before she had time to alter the will again. Black as this was, however, he must again ask them not to allow it to weigh too much with them. The prisoner might have desired her death, yet the last thing he would be guilty of might be the causing of her death. He did not see much controversy between the doctors. He had listened to all that was said by Dr Farquharson, but after all there was very little difference in it. Dr Farquharson's evidence could not have much weight, although he did propound a different theory – that the woman had had a diseased brain and might have fallen in a fit. This doctor, when asked, could only speak of one previous case strangulation in his experience, and when a medical man gave evidence in that way, he thought it was not very reliable and was more theory.

As to the evidence of the prisoner being in the house at the time, it was overwhelming that he was there. Had there been any suggestion that anybody else was there? That somebody was assaulting her in the house, there was no doubt - the evidence was not only of shouts but of cries of "Dinna dee it, dinna dee it" and so on.

"If there is this strong evidence," his lordship asked, "that the prisoner was there and what was done was done by him, it is a matter for you, the only duty of the Judge is to draw attention to the effect of the evidence given. If you find on the evidence that the prisoner was there – what happened we cannot tell except the result of what was done by somebody – you have to consider what that points to and as to who did it."

Another extraordinary thing was the finding

of the remains, under the grate, of the corsets she was wearing. If they were burnt on the body, they would have been found on the body. Who put them where they were found? Nobody else but the prisoner was there, and if they were put there by anybody it was by the prisoner. He did not see how it could have been possible if the whole thing was accidental. As to the blind being drawn down, no theory was suggested as to what could induce the woman to draw it.

Judge Grantham then dealt with Matt Dodds' conduct, saying: "It does seem to me to be about as heartless as it is possible to imagine. Let us assume he was innocent: what would be the conduct of an innocent man having lost his wife by the painful death of burning? Do you think he would have simply gone to somebody and said "My wife's been found dead", not asked for anyone to go for a doctor, or telegraphed for one. He never did anything. When the people come there, he goes not even to the room but stands by the door – exactly the same when the doctor does come when telegraphed for. He does nothing.

"But there was something he did and said which was very significant. It was the great anxiety he had speaking to the constable – that the inquest should be held as soon as possible. Why should he be so anxious about the inquest? You would have thought there was every desire to find out everything that had occurred. There is no doubt it was a great advantage to him having it the next day because the inquiry was rushed in a way it ought not to have been." It was hardly likely that the woman had died from what was suggested by the prisoner. It was remarkable that he should have stated that which had nothing to confirm it.

His lordship then further asked if there had been any suggestions as to how, if she had been drawn away from the fire, any accidental tightening of the shawl could have remained tight? Assuming it was accidental, the moment the position of the body was altered, that accidental tightness would go. If the jury thought the woman was strangled by the prisoner, was not the inference almost irresistible that, having caused her death, he was desirous of preventing it being discovered and then placed her over the cinders? If they thought there was a rational or reasonable doubt, by all means let them give the prisoner the benefit of it, but if they thought the evidence was too strong, no matter how painful it might be to them, they must do their duty.

On concluding his summing-up, Mr Justice Grantham then asked the jury to retire to consider their verdict, and the court was adjourned for an hour.

Chapter 13

Matt waited in his cell, the bread and water provided for him by the warder untouched on the bench beside him. His mind was numb, the events of the last two days spinning out of control in his brain. Outwardly though, he maintained the *sangfroid* and calm that he had displayed throughout.

He placed his head in his hands and thought of his father and brother. He had been unable to pick them out within the crowd in the public gallery, but he was certain they had been there. He wondered how his father was coping through all of this; he was an old man now and Matt felt sure this must be taking a terrible toll upon him. A wave of remorse swept over him as he thought of the distress he had caused his father. His one consolation was knowing that his brother would take care of him whatever happened.

Michael Dodds was waiting outside in Old Elvet, standing slightly apart from the throng who had piled out of the courthouse and listening to their excited speculation as they went over the evidence and tried to anticipate the verdict of the jury. Throughout the trial, Michael had occupied one of the hard wooden benches at the back of the public gallery, his eyes fixed on the person of his son, as he listened to every minute detail of the case. Matt, he was proud to see, remained motionless throughout, his pale face showing no emotion, maintaining his dignity. Michael wondered why they had not given him a chair, aware that standing for that length of time would have been agony for his crippled son.

How much of this was Michael's own fault? That was the question he couldn't get out of his mind. Maybe he had been too hard on Matt, aware as he had been of the way the other children taunted him as a boy. He had known that his crippled son was going to have to be tough to survive, and would have to fight his own battles. He would have to learn that life owed him no favours. Was he wrong to have discouraged his mother from mollycoddling him, protecting him from the harsh realities of village life? And then as he grew older, should he have tried to bring him out of himself more, encouraged him to join in more instead of hiding away in his shed with his woodwork?

But Matt had proved himself to be a hard worker, reliable, and you had to admire him tramping across the Fell to Cockfield in all weathers for all those years and never complaining. He was skilled in the joinery shop too, and Michael had always assumed he and Charlie would take over the business when the time came. Then when Matt had got on with Mary Jane, he had been pleased, happy for him that he had found someone to share his life with. Oh, he wasn't daft, he had known that the marriage wasn't a happy one, he had heard the rumours and gossip in the village. And yes, he had seen the black eyes and the cuts and bruises. But this? He just couldn't get his head around it. Was his son really capable of murdering his wife in such a cruel and heartless way? He was only glad that Matt's mother was not here to have witnessed all of this.

The crowd began to move towards the big entrance door to the court and Michael, breathing deeply to steady his nerves, walked slowly back and took his place on the bench beside his son Charlie at the back of the public gallery. Matt was already back in the dock, his face ashen, but he still seemed to be bearing himself well. Michael tried to catch his eye, but the angle was not right.

The court stood as the members of the jury came in and took up their places before Mr Justice Grantham entered through a side door and climbed to his high seat above them all. The clerk called for order and a silent anticipation descended on the court. Matt firmly gripped the railings in front of him with both hands, swaying only slightly as the clerk asked the foreman of the jury to stand and asked if they had come to a verdict.

"We have," the foreman replied.

"How do you find the prisoner, Matthew James Dodds, guilty or not guilty?"

"Guilty," the foreman announced.

A loud collective gasp from the public benches filled the air, causing the clerk to remind everyone of their need to keep silent. Mr Justice Grantham turned to Matt and asked him if he had anything to say as to why judgement should not be passed upon him. In a firm, clear voice Matt simply replied: "Well, I am not guilty, sir."

Mr Justice Grantham then placed a black cap over his white wig and in a solemn voice pronounced: "Matthew James Dodds, the jury have found you guilty of wilful murder and I am quite sure the verdict they have passed is the only verdict in accordance with the evidence. No one who has heard the evidence should honestly come to any other conclusion. It is not for me to aggravate the painful position in which you must feel placed at the present time, nor is it necessary for me to go into any causes which may have caused you or induced you to do this. I have only to perform the duty cast upon me, and that is to pass upon you sentence of death. You will be taken from this place to a prison and thence to a place of execution and you will then be hanged by the neck until dead and your body will be buried in the precincts of the gaol. May God have mercy on your soul."

At the pronouncement of the verdict all mayhem broke out in the public gallery, with some people jumping up from their seats, shouting and gesticulating, whilst others remained as they were, speechless, in a state of shock. Michael struggled to his feet and desperately tried to push through the melee to catch sight of his son. Clambering over the benches he reached the front of the gallery and yelled Matt's name across the court room. He could see Matt standing stock still as a warder was placing his hands into handcuffs.

Michael shouted again and Matt turned, their eyes meeting fleetingly across the room before he was led away down the steep steps to the tunnel and back to his cell. Michael sank to his knees, all his steely determination to be strong through this deserting him. He felt every one of his seventy years as there came over him the feeling that his life, along with his son's, was now over. He couldn't see how he was going to carry on. Loud, deep sobs racking his old, lean body.

Then he was aware of firm, strong hands lifting him to his feet, and Charlie's voice urging him: "Come on Dad, get up. We have to go home. There's nothing more we can do here."

Charlie steered his father out of the courthouse and into the cool of the evening. Avoiding the eyes of those already in the street and pushing away the offers of sympathy, he virtually carried him back the station. The two stared in silence through the carriage window on the return train journey, their fellow passengers speaking in hushed, stunned whispers, all the gaiety and high spirits of two days earlier now gone.

Matt meanwhile, his status now having changed, was being escorted by two warders to the condemned cell on the Prison's "A" Wing. He was surprised to find it quite spacious, his professional eye noting that it had been formed from two single cells being knocked into one. Along one wall was the standard prison bed and against the opposite wall a small wooden table and bench. Across one corner were two simple wooden shelves on which there were placed a bowl, plate and cup. In the opposite corner was the usual metal bucket and beside it a small, three-legged stool. The window was in the usual place, high up on the wall, but Matt noted with a shiver that its six small panes had heavy iron bars attached to the outside.

Matt's condemned status also meant that the Prison Governor, Mr J Dillon, now had personal responsibility for his security and safety and to this end he had arranged for him to be kept under observation, with a warder in the cell with him at all times, day and night.

The Governor was a kindly man who took his

responsibility seriously, so he made a point of visiting Matt in his cell each day, keeping him well-informed as to the progress of his particular situation. Even so, it came as something of a surprise when Governor Dillon came into Matt's cell a few days after his conviction and, sitting himself on the three-legged stool, explained to him that there had been an interesting development in his case. He had heard personally from Mr Short that he intended to take full advantage on Matt's behalf of the Criminal Appeals Act which had recently passed into law. Seeing the blank look on Matt's face, the Governor explained in as simple terms as he could that the previous year had seen a change in the law, meaning that those found guilty in criminal cases such as his could now make an appeal. Mr Short intended to launch such an appeal against Matt's conviction and sentence, which was due to be heard in front of the Lord Chief Justice and two High Court Judges on the 17th of July, four days before the date set for his execution. Mr Short intended to put forward the argument that in his opinion that there was a flaw in the summing up by the Judge, Mr Justice Grantham, and that evidence had not been called at the trial to support Matt's claim that he had been away from the house at the time, this being a crucial part of his defence.

The next few days found Matt in a state of tense expectation. He understood little about the procedure which was to be undertaken on his behalf and he hardly dare allow himself the luxury of thinking it might be successful. He occupied his time reading the daily newspaper and writing letters to his father and brother and to friends in Hamsterley. The Chaplain came to see him each day to pray with him and attend to his spiritual needs and the Governor also did his best to keep him in good spirits and optimistic of the outcome of the appeal.

On the evening of the 17th however, Governor Dillon came to his cell with news of the appeal made by Mr Short, which had been sent to the Criminal Court of Appeal accompanied by a petition which contained nearly two thousand signatures. The Governor had in his hand a letter which he had received that day, and in a solemn voice, he read out to Matt: *"Sir – I am directed by the Secretary of State to acquaint you that, having had under consideration the case of Matthew James Dodds, now lying under sentence of death in Durham Prison, he has failed to discover any sufficient ground to justify him in advising His Majesty to interfere with the due course of the law, I am, sir, your obedient servant, E. Blackwell."*

The Appeal Panel had ruled that there was nothing wrong in the summing-up given by the Judge and that the evidence presented in court had been strong enough for the jury to return the guilty verdict. It was therefore, Mr Dillon's painful duty to inform Matt that his execution had now been set to take place on the 5th of August.

Matt sat in silence on the bench beside the little table with his eyes cast to the floor of the cell as the Governor read out the letter. He made no reply. As the Governor walked down the corridor away from the condemned man's cell, a rich, baritone voice reached him, singing the words of a well- known hymn:

What peaceful hours I once enjoyed!
How sweet their memory still!
But they have left an aching void
The world can never fill.

Chapter 14

During the final three weeks of his life Matt remained relatively cheerful and continued to keep himself busy. The Governor, being a kindly and sympathetic man, granted him permission to receive visitors in his cell. These included a couple of close friends who made the journey to Durham from Hamsterley bringing with them news of the village and the good wishes of the villagers, with the visit from his father and brother Charlie being perhaps the most poignant. During all of these visits, Matt remained positive and cheerful, doing his best to comfort and reassure everyone and urging them not to fret about him. He repeatedly reassured those who came to see him of his total innocence and that, therefore, he had nothing to fear from death.

He continued to write to family and friends during these final days of his life; in all his letters he urged their recipients not to be fearful for him, assuring them that he was well and not afraid of death. Continuing to claim his innocence of any wrongdoing, his letters often had a strong religious theme, saying he was confident that someone would pay for what had happened, either in this life or the next.

One such letter was to Mr Harry Gripps, a farmer who now lived near West Auckland but who had formerly been the Landlord of the Cross Keys.

Dear Sir, I was very sorry I could not have a word with you at the Court. I am keeping fairly well under the circumstances I am in. I appealed against my case and the appeal went against me so there seems to be nothing else but death for me now. Well Harry, I am very sorry I am in such a position, but I can honestly say I am an innocent man. It has been an accident in some form or other. She was alright when I left her and it will not be revealed until we meet around the Throne of God as to how it happened. I am expecting my father, Charlie (sic), William and Mrs Henderson to see me on Wednesday. I thank you very kindly for coming through to Durham. Do your best for me.

You will be very busy with your hay as we are having very fine weather at present. I hope you have good crops this season. The Governor, chaplain and other officials have been very kind and good in helping me in my great trouble for which I feel grateful for their kindness and comfort. Give my best respects to your wife and family, also Anthony Oates and others.

I draw to a close – from your innocent friend.

MATTHEW J DODDS

PS Love to all. "In the midst of life we are in death".

He also wrote to his friend William Henderson:

Dear William, I received your letter and was very glad to hear from you as it does me a great deal of good to hear from my friend. Well William, I am keeping well and bearing up and in good heart. The last key on this bunch has not opened the lock for my reprieve, so there is nothing but death for me now. But I have nothing to be afraid of to meet death, as I am prepared for it and I have a clear conscience and can honestly and truly say I am innocent of the crime I am condemned for. But there will be a few called to account for my life when they come before the Great Judge of all men, when the truth will be proved. It has been an accident in some form or other.

While I have been here my mind has often wandered back to the pleasant walks and rides I often used to have, but they are all over now.

Well shortly after you receive this letter I will have been launched out of time into eternity. There is going to be prayer for me in the mission room on my behalf. I hope you or your missus will go and help to give me a lift up into the Heavenly City where all will be bright and beautiful and where there will be no more trouble or trial or sorrow, but where we shall enjoy the pleasure and blessings of God for ever. I am only going a little while before the rest. It seems very hard that I have had to come to an end of this kind but we cannot make better of it now.

So I conclude with my last loving farewell to all friends and your wife and family and yourself. Good-bye until we meet again where there will be no more parting.

From your innocent friend MATTHEW J. DODDS

"In the midst of life we are in death."

Good-bye.

On the 3rd of August Matt wrote once again to John Heads, thanking his friend for a letter which had cheered him up a good deal. As a reprieve had not been granted him, there was nothing but death for him now. He repeated his statement that he had nothing to fear from death and that his conscience was clear, and said that someone would be called to account about his life when they came before the 'great judge of all men', when the truth would be proved. He went on to speak of a visit he had had from his father and brother, saying that his father could not stay long as he had felt it so much to see him in such a position. He told John that his tools had been left at the pit and suggested he might buy them and send his father what he thought they were worth as he had some outstanding bills to be paid. He thanked John for helping with the petition and thanked him also for how he had spoken about his character. He had, he said, always tried to be respectable and kind and cheerful with everybody and do the best he could in this world.

He told John of his regret at not having been able to see him before he parted from this world as he would have liked to have had a little chat with him about the case. He ended with words from the hymn "What peaceful hours I once enjoyed" and added "only going a little time before".

On the evening of the 4th of August, Matt sat at the little wooden table in his cell and began to write his final letter to his father and brother:

Dear father and brother, It is a great pleasure to me to write these few lines to you to try and cheer and comfort you in this great trouble we are going through. Do keep up your heart and don't fret about me. As I told you before, I am quite innocent and have nothing to be afraid of to meet death. I will be far better off when I reach Heaven City, when all trouble and sorrow will then be over and to be with those who have gone before and enjoy the pleasure for evermore. And never for one moment think I am anything else but innocent. If I hadn't been, I would have confessed to you like a man before I parted from this world. If you can believe me, your son Matt, I told the truth about the case... He then referred to letters he had received and visits paid to him by friends, as well as mentioning again the kindness shown by the Governor, chaplain and prison officials. ... *Well dear father, put your trust in the One above and you will find in Him a great help and comfort for the remainder of your years... shortly after you receive this letter, I will have been launched out of time into eternity to be with God and His redeemed One, around His Throne to sing His praises. I conclude with my last, loving farewell to you and Charlie and all friends.*

From your innocent and true son, MATTHEW JAMES DODDS.

To his brother he added:

Dear Charlie
I ask you kindly to look after and be kind to father, and take care of yourself in your future life. I am only going a little while before the rest.

Chapter 15

As Matt was writing his farewell letter, two men stepped from their train in Durham Station and hailed a cab to take them the short distance to the prison. They were the brothers Henry and Thomas Pierrepoint, members of the infamous family of executioners, who had been chosen for the hanging by the High Sheriff of Durham from the Home Office list of approved executioners. Both men had extensive experience, having between them carried out, or assisted at, a great number of hangings throughout the land, and as such they were no strangers to Durham.

At precisely four o'clock, in accordance with the legal requirement, they were admitted to the prison and accompanied by the Governor and the Prison Doctor, they were escorted to the condemned cell, where they had their first sight of Matt, who respectfully stood as the party entered the cell. "How are you, Matt?" the Governor asked. "All right, sir," he replied.

Henry Pierrepoint, who had been designated as the hangman with his brother assisting, looked intensely at Matt, taking in his appearance before asking the doctor for details of his height and weight. He then paid close attention to Matt's crippled leg and thought for a few moments before carefully recording all the details in his diary in his neat, meticulous writing. Henry Pierrepoint had a reputation for taking great pride in his work and was known to calculate the drops most carefully. He had never been known to bungle a single hanging.

Matt of course was unaware of all of this, but as he watched the hangman make his careful measurements and calculations, he had the sense that he was at least in the hands of a professional.

Henry then stepped forward and held out his hand to Matt, who after a moment's hesitation, firmly shook it before the hangman left the cell without a word being exchanged between the two of them.

Matt's night, his last, was long with only snatches of sleep. The young warder on duty tried to keep the atmosphere light by talking about anything and everything, but with the gaps between their conversations getting longer, he was at a loss as to what to say to the condemned man.

Meanwhile in the execution shed in the prison yard, the Pierrepoint brothers were making their careful calculations. The fact of Matt's crippled leg was posing them something of a problem; neither man had ever hanged a cripple before. The governor observed their work carefully, conscious of his responsibility to ensure that all the equipment was put up correctly, and he watched as the gallows was erected over the pit.

Finally, satisfied that all was in order, the two executioners retired to spend the night in the warder's quarters.

Slowly the new day dawned over a sleepy Durham City and shafts of light found their way through the high window and into Matt's cell. In the street outside a small crowd had gathered, shivering slightly in the cold early morning air. Some were just curious bystanders, but among them were several from Hamsterley who had travelled into the city on the milk train. Standing apart, with his hands deep in his coat pockets and his eyes cast to the ground, was Charlie Dodds, determined to be as near to his brother in his final moments as was possible.

At six o'clock the warder's shift ended and, not knowing what else to do, he shook Matt's hand and left without saying goodbye. Two new warders came into the cell, men Matt had not seen before; his last hour on earth was to be spent with strangers.

Matt's breakfast of bread, butter and tea arrived as usual and although his stomach was turning somersaults, he somehow felt it his duty to eat it. On the instructions of Henry Pierrepoint, he was now wearing an open-necked, blue-striped prison shirt, grey trousers and grey felt slippers. The chaplain and the doctor arrived, closely followed by the governor and the Lord Lieutenant of the county. In a gesture to calm his nerves, Matt was offered a large tot of whisky, which he refused, keeping to his Non-Conformist principles to the end.

The last to enter the cell were the two executioners, and with them the atmosphere in the cell intensified as the hangmen put into practice their well-rehearsed procedures. Matt was instructed to stand up and the two warders who had spent the last hour with him took up position on either side of the condemned man. Henry Pierrepoint, looking Matt straight in the eye, assured him that it would all be very quick and easy. Thomas Pierrepoint then went behind Matt and expertly secured his arms behind his back with a leather belt. The warders then took an arm each and escorted Matt, who walked in as dignified a way as his crippled leg would allow, out from the condemned cell and into the long corridor which led to the execution shed.

The melancholy procession walked swiftly along its length, headed by the Governor and the High Sheriff, with the robed Chaplain in quiet, measured tones reading the words from the Burial Service. Behind Matt and the two warders were the two executioners, Thomas carrying a white cap and the straps which he was to use to fasten the Matt's legs. Bringing up the rear, at a short distance, walked a representative of the press. The shed was quite a small, wooden structure and bizarrely the joiner in Matt couldn't help noticing the poor quality of the workmanship of its construction; it was obviously a temporary structure.

They entered through the narrow door and the two warders took up their positions on beams either side of the trap doors and held on to braided ropes. Matt was then gently guided onto the closed trapdoors and at that moment Thomas Pierrepoint squatted behind him and fastened the leather straps around his legs. Henry Pierrepoint then placed a white hood and rope together over the condemned man's head. He turned the rope so the knot was at the side of Matt's neck and then took up the slack. Wordlessly the hangman stepped back and the only sound was that of the Chaplain's voice as he continued his prayers.

Henry Pierrepoint then placed a hand on the lever which operated the trap, and gave a signal to the warders, who released Matt's arms. For barely a second Matt stood on the trapdoors, bound, blindfolded and isolated. In the silent darkness of the hood, he knew all too well what was about to happen. As the nearby Assize Court's clock began striking the hour, Henry Pierrepoint pulled the lever and without a sound Matt plummeted the length of the drop and was launched into eternity.

As the clock finished striking, the prison bell began to toll, at which point all those present left the execution shed and it was then locked behind them. Matt's body was left hanging in the execution shed for the customary hour and the

Governor then gave instructions for the official notice of the execution to be posted on the prison gate.

Later in the morning, as the law required, a formal coroner's inquest was held within the confines of the prison. It was presided over by the County Coroner, with a jury in attendance and before which the prison governor, the prison doctor and the senior warder all gave evidence to confirm the identity of the deceased and give account of the day's events. Satisfied with his findings, the Coroner recorded that death had occurred through judicial hanging and released Matt's body for burial within the prison grounds.

Later that day, once the sun had set, Matt's body, dressed only in a plain shirt and laid in a pine coffin, was carried by four warders, accompanied only by the Governor and the Chaplain to a plot beside the prison wall. The grave remained unmarked, a simple entry in the prison's records showing its location.

In Hamsterley a deep sense of shock and sadness had descended over the village. The reality of the events which had occurred over the past few months was beginning to sink in. The newspapers had carried detailed accounts of the trial and execution and those villagers unable to travel to Durham had pored over every little detail in them, marvelling at the attention the case was drawing. There was even a certain macabre pride amongst them to see their village so prominently featured and to see the names of people they knew in print.

Now, however, the reporters had moved on to the next big story. The newspapers were now full of reports of the increased activities and mass meetings of the Suffragettes and news was coming through of a 'great storm' which had caused unprecedented damage along the South Wales coast.

As to Mary Jane's properties, the court ruled that her cousin Margaret should inherit them, as had been her former wish. Life in the village gradually went back to normal, but Michael Dodds returned to his little joinery shop with a heavy heart.

One afternoon towards the end of August, a stranger came into the workshop who did not look to Michael like someone in need of a blade sharpening. The man introduced himself as a warder from Durham Prison and explained that he was there on an errand on behalf of the Governor, Mr Dillon. He then handed Michael a parcel wrapped in plain brown paper and with it a handwritten note.

The old man looked at the parcel for some time as if in a trance before slowing unwrapping the paper. Inside was a little hardback book and Michael stared at it for some minutes. The title, written clearly in bold letters, read:

"Two Words, Did It"
(and other narratives)

Michael continued to stare at the book for a further few minutes before opening it to the first page, on which was written in Matt's neat handwriting:

August 1908
Presented to Michael John Dodds
From his son,
Matthew James Dodds

Seeing the tears begin to fall down the old man's cheeks, the warden quietly left the workshop, closing the door behind him.

Epilogue

Michael John Dodds continued to live in Hamsterley until his death on December 29th 1924 aged 83 years. He was buried in Hamsterley Baptist churchyard on March 2nd 1925 alongside his wife Hannah, son John Robert and infant daughters Annie and Nancy. Presumably the delay between his death and the burial was due to the harsh winter weather. Charlie (Charles Henry) Dodds remained, unmarried, in Hamsterley, running a small sawmill. He died in 1954 aged 76 years and was also buried in the Baptist churchyard on 2nd of April of that year. Michael John's other son, George (1872- 1948?) is recorded on the 1911 Census as living in Bishop Auckland with his wife Margaret (*née* Walton) and two small children. He gives his occupation as being a coal miner.

Matthew James' grandfather, Matthew Dodds (1812-1885), and my husband Ian's great-great grandfather John Dodds (1814-1870) were brothers and two of the sons of William Dodds (1772-1862) who began the edge-tool making business in Bedburn. John Dodds' son is the John Dodds who was accosted by ruffians alongside Jack Marquis.

Jack Marquis' grocery shop and the archway which separated it from Mary Jane's house have since been converted into the restaurant of the Cross Keys Inn.

The full reasons behind the suicide of Jack Marquis can only be speculated upon. The inquest heard he suffered from bouts of depression and the incident with young
John Dove seems to suggest a slight imbalance in his reasoning. It may also be the case that his business was in difficulties; after all these were

hard times and the population of the village for the most part was poor. The fact that Mary Jane was forced to take legal action following his death to retrieve unpaid bills certainly suggests that. Did he possibly resent the time Mary Jane spent with her mother? There is no indication that the relationship between Jack and Mary Jane was violent, and it remains unknown as to what extent their drinking played a part.

There is no evidence that Matthew Dodds displayed any tendency towards violence in the years prior to his marriage to Mary Jane. He appears to have been well-liked and his family respected within the community. It is also evident that the families were close and indeed interrelated, Matt having known Mary Jane all of his life. Therefore, the reasons behind their troubled marriage can only be deduced from the evidence presented at the trial. It is clear however that their short marriage seems to have been in trouble from the start.

Also, to the present-day reader, it may appear strange, if not incomprehensible, that the villagers were obviously fully aware of the violence that occurred between Matt and Mary Jane but chose to ignore it. However, views on domestic violence were very different at this time and were rooted in the inequality between men and women in society. Abuse towards a wife was viewed as being a normal part of marriage, even something that women should expect and tolerate. The general attitude was that whatever occurred between husband and wife was a private matter. This seems also to have been the attitude of the police as evidenced in PC Lowe taking no action when called to the incident outside the couple's house despite Mary Jane's accusations.

When looking at the trial we must resist the temptation to impose present-day methods and medical and forensic knowledge. The scientific and medical experts who were called to give evidence were from the highest level of their professions at that time. The fact that the shawl around Mary Jane's neck was either not noticed initially or not considered of importance does seem questionable, however.

It is interesting to note here that the trial judge, Mr Justice William Grantham, appears to have been a man with a reputation for making comments during cases. In 1911, he was rebuked in the House of Commons by Prime Minister Asquith over an indiscreet speech to the jury at a trial in Liverpool.

The evidence given by the neighbours and villagers is interesting and does I think reflect the close-knit "gossipy" nature of every -day life in the village. It seems that everyone knew each other's business and where they were at any given time in the day. The contradictions in the details between the evidence given at the inquest and at the trial give us some indication of the conversations and discussions which must inevitably have taken place in the intervening time. Throughout his trial Matt remained unwavering in his claim to innocence, insisting throughout that he was not in the house at the time. His letters to family and friends are poignant and bear witness to his Baptist faith, there being many scriptural references and quotations.

Matthew James was the first man under sentence of death to appeal under the new Criminal Appeal Act of 1907, a procedure which went all the way to the House of Lords. It remained the highest court in England until 2009 when it was replaced by the Supreme Court.

The Pierrepoints are worth a mention as they were a renowned family of executioners. Henry was made the official executioner for Britain in 1905 and persuaded his brother Thomas to join the family business. His son Albert, inspired by his father, also took up the family trade. Henry's career came to an abrupt end however when in 1910, only two years after executing Matthew James, he was removed from the official list of executioners when the day before an execution at Chelmsford he had arrived "considerably the worse for drink" and got into a fight with his assistant, John Ellis.

Thomas Pierrepoint was ten years older than his brother and was a hangman for forty years. He was the official executioner for the Irish republic following its independence from

England and was responsible for the hanging of sixteen US servicemen at Shepton Mallet during the Second World War.

Finally, we come to the enigma of the book sent to Michael John Dodds with its strange and revealing title, the delivery of which was reported in the newspaper coverage of the trial. I have been unable to find any reference to such a book being presently in print. I can only speculate as to how Matt managed to obtain it whilst in prison; presumably he enlisted the help of a family member or someone within the prison. Do we finally have a confession here? Or is it an attempt to ease his father's pain, allowing him to think that at least his son did not die as an innocent man? We will never know.

My title, "Shabby Wedding", takes me back to my childhood when we would walk the fields and meadows around the village in the North-East where I grew up and gather the seeds of the dock plant by pulling our fingers and thumbs up the long stems. We would then chase after each other throwing the seeds, mimicking a poor person's confetti, to the chant of "Shabby weddin', shabby weddin'!" The word "shabby" in northern parlance equates with poor, down at heel or scruffy as well as hinting at something being dishonourable, shameful or mean-spirited. It seems a fitting description of Matt and Mary Jane's marriage.

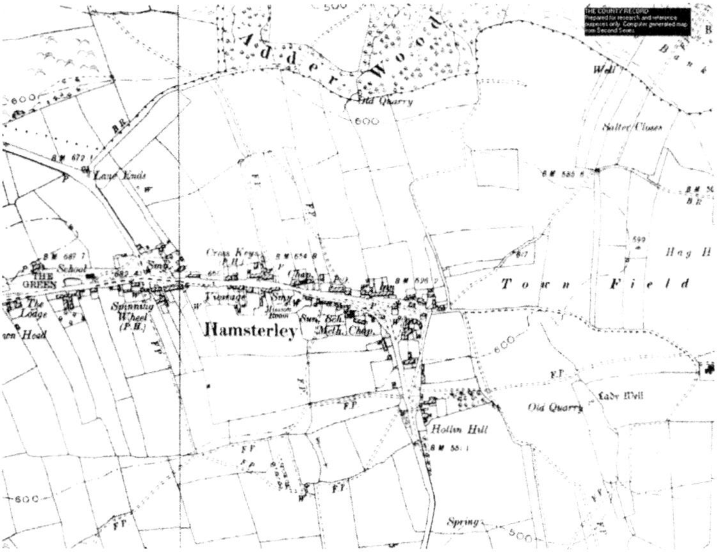

An 1898 map of Hamsterley showing the Cross Keys public house in the centre of the village

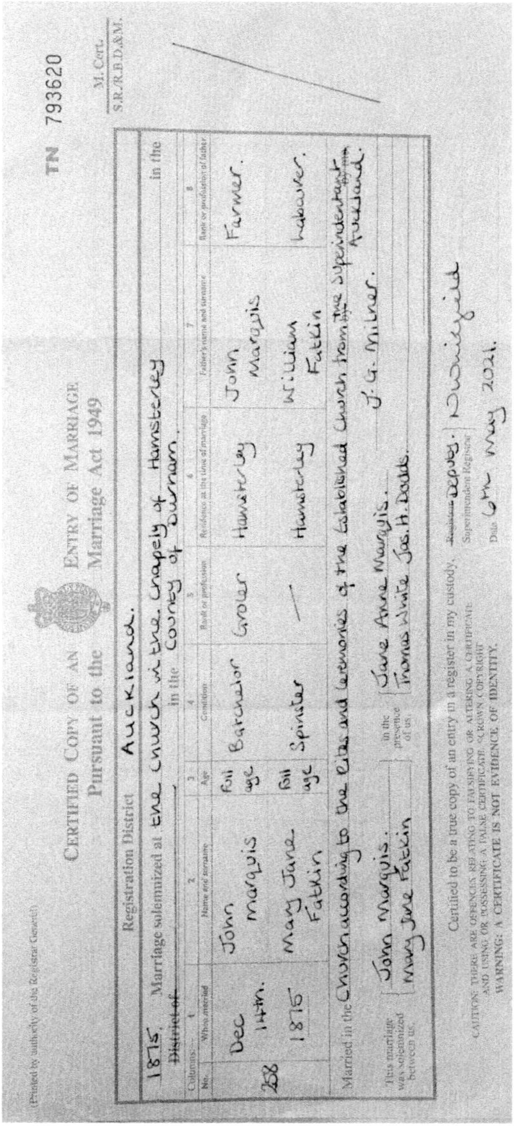

(Printed by authority of the Registrar General)

TN 793620

M. Cert.
S.R./R.B.D.&M.

CERTIFIED COPY OF AN ENTRY OF MARRIAGE
Pursuant to the Marriage Act 1949

Registration District Auckland.

1875. Marriage solemnized at the church in the Chapely of Hamsterley in the ~~District of~~ in the County of Durnam.

Columns:— 1 No.	1 When married	2 Name and surname	3 Age	4 Condition	5 Rank or profession	6 Residence at the time of marriage	7 Father's name and surname	8 Rank or profession of father
258	Dec 14th. 1875	John Marquis	Full age	Batchelor	Groler	Hamsterley	John Marquis	Farmer.
		Mary Jane Fatkin	Full age	Spinster	—	Hamsterley	William Fatkin	Labourer.

Married in the Church according to the Rites and Ceremonies of the Established Church from the Superintendant ~~by me~~ Auckland.

J. G. Milner.

This marriage was solemnized between us, John Marquis. Mary Jane Fatkin

in the presence of us, Jane Anne Marquis. Thomas White Jas. H. Dodds.

Certified to be a true copy of an entry in a register in my custody. ~~Registrar~~ Deputy. Superintendent Registrar

Date 6th May 2021.

CAUTION: THERE ARE OFFENCES RELATING TO FALSIFYING OR ALTERING A CERTIFICATE AND USING OR POSSESSING A FALSE CERTIFICATE. ©CROWN COPYRIGHT
WARNING: A CERTIFICATE IS NOT EVIDENCE OF IDENTITY.

Marriage certificate of John Marquis and Mary Jane Fatkin, December 1875.

FE 923343

CERTIFIED COPY of an ENTRY
Pursuant to the Births and Deaths Registration Act 1953

1891 Registration District Auckland

Death in the Sub-district of Hamsterley in the County of Durham

Columns:-	1	2	3	4	5	6	7	8	9
No.	When and where died	Name and surname	Sex	Age	Occupation	Cause of death	Signature, description, and residence of informant	When registered	Signature of registrar
263	Twenty second May 1891 Hamsterley RSD	John Marquis	Male	45 years	Grocer	Suicide by hanging whilst temporarily insane	Certificate received from Thomas Dean Coroner for Darlington Ward Inquest held Twenty third May 1891	Twenty fifth May 1891	JE Townsend Registrar

Certified to be a true copy of an entry in a register in my custody.

N Wingfield Deputy Superintendent Registrar

6.5.2021 Date

CAUTION: THERE ARE OFFENCES RELATING TO FALSIFYING OR ALTERING A CERTIFICATE AND USING OR POSSESSING A FALSE CERTIFICATE. ©CROWN COPYRIGHT

WARNING: A CERTIFICATE IS NOT EVIDENCE OF IDENTITY.

Death Certificate of John Marquis, 1891.

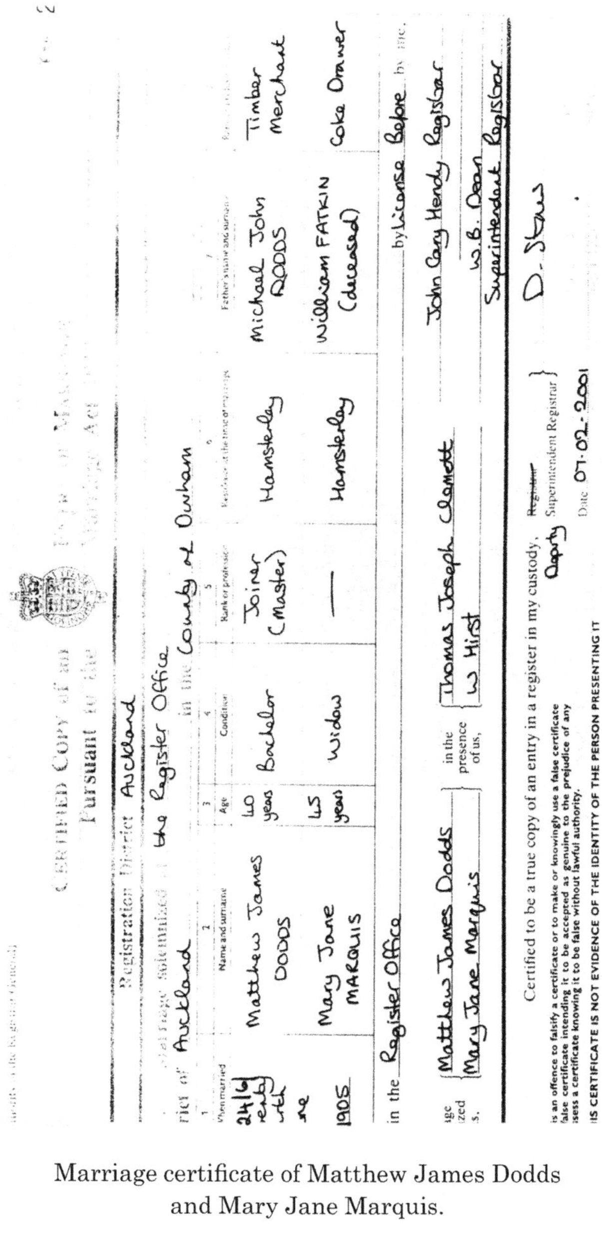

CERTIFIED COPY of an ... Pursuant to the ... Act

Registration District Auckland

... solemnized at the Register Office in the ... of Auckland in the County of Durham

When married	Name and surname	Age	Condition	Rank or profession	Residence at the time of marriage	Father's name and surname	Rank or profession of father
24/6 1905	Matthew James DODDS	40 years	Bachelor	Joiner (Master)	Hamsterley	Michael John DODDS	Timber Merchant
	Mary Jane MARQUIS	45 years	Widow	—	Hamsterley	William FATKIN (deceased)	Coke Drawer

... in the Register Office by licence Before by me,

Matthew James Dodds / Mary Jane Marquis — in the presence of us, Thomas Joseph Clemett / W Hirst — John Cary Hendy Registrar / W.B. Dean Superintendent Registrar

Certified to be a true copy of an entry in a register in my custody. Deputy Superintendent Registrar

Date 07.02.2001

... is an offence to falsify a certificate or to make or knowingly use a false certificate ... false certificate intending it to be accepted as genuine to the prejudice of any ... possess a certificate knowing it to be false without lawful authority.

... THIS CERTIFICATE IS NOT EVIDENCE OF THE IDENTITY OF THE PERSON PRESENTING IT

Marriage certificate of Matthew James Dodds and Mary Jane Marquis.

The Cross Keys, Hamsterley, showing the adjacent grocer's shop and the archway through to the rear lane. The Dodd's house can be seen behind the archway, clearly showing the side door.

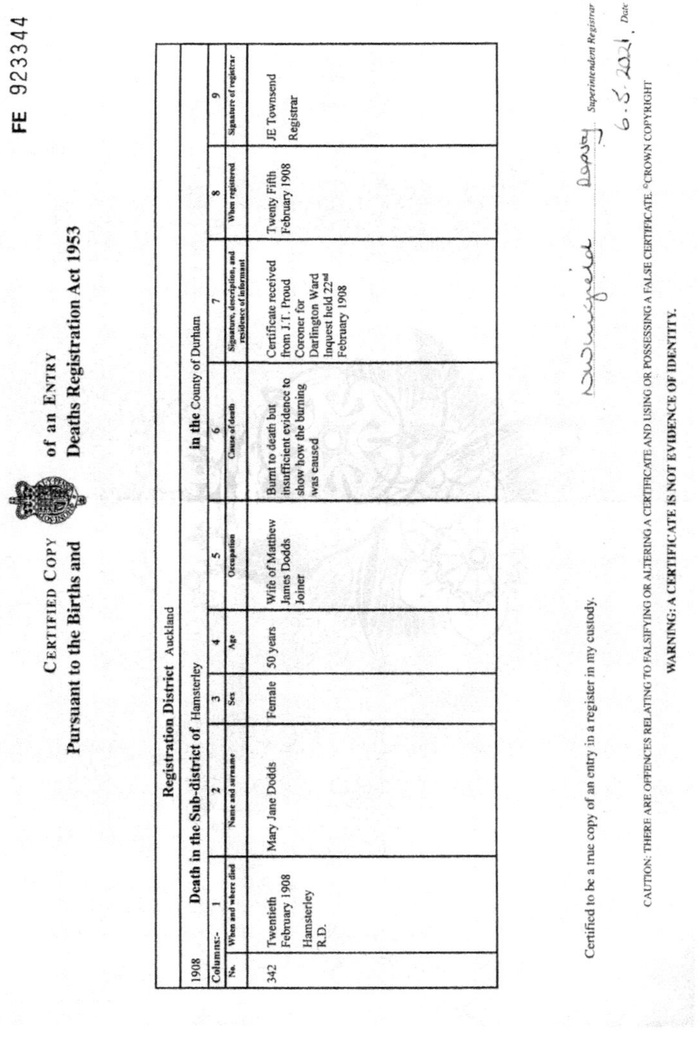

FE 923344

CERTIFIED COPY of an ENTRY
Pursuant to the Births and Deaths Registration Act 1953

Registration District Auckland

1908 Death in the Sub-district of Hamsterley in the County of Durham

Columns:-	1	2	3	4	5	6	7	8	9
No.	When and where died	Name and surname	Sex	Age	Occupation	Cause of death	Signature, description, and residence of informant	When registered	Signature of registrar
342	Twentieth February 1908 Hamsterley R.D.	Mary Jane Dodds	Female	50 years	Wife of Matthew James Dodds Joiner	Burnt to death but insufficient evidence to show how the burning was caused	Certificate received from J.T. Proud Coroner for Darlington Ward Inquest held 22nd February 1908	Twenty Fifth February 1908	JE Townsend Registrar

Certified to be a true copy of an entry in a register in my custody.

Superintendent Registrar

6.5.2021 Date

CAUTION: THERE ARE OFFENCES RELATING TO FALSIFYING OR ALTERING A CERTIFICATE AND USING OR POSSESSING A FALSE CERTIFICATE. ©CROWN COPYRIGHT

WARNING: A CERTIFICATE IS NOT EVIDENCE OF IDENTITY.

Death certificate of Mary Jane Dodds, giving the cause as 'burnt to death'. This was not changed after the trial.

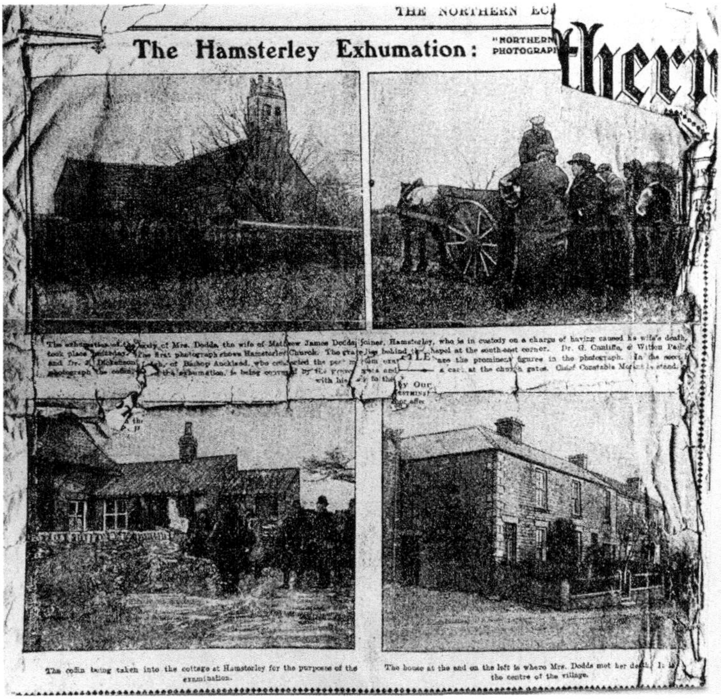

The grainy photographs of the exhumation which appeared in the *Northern Echo*.

A court artist's drawing of Matthew James Dodds which appeared in the *Northern Echo.*

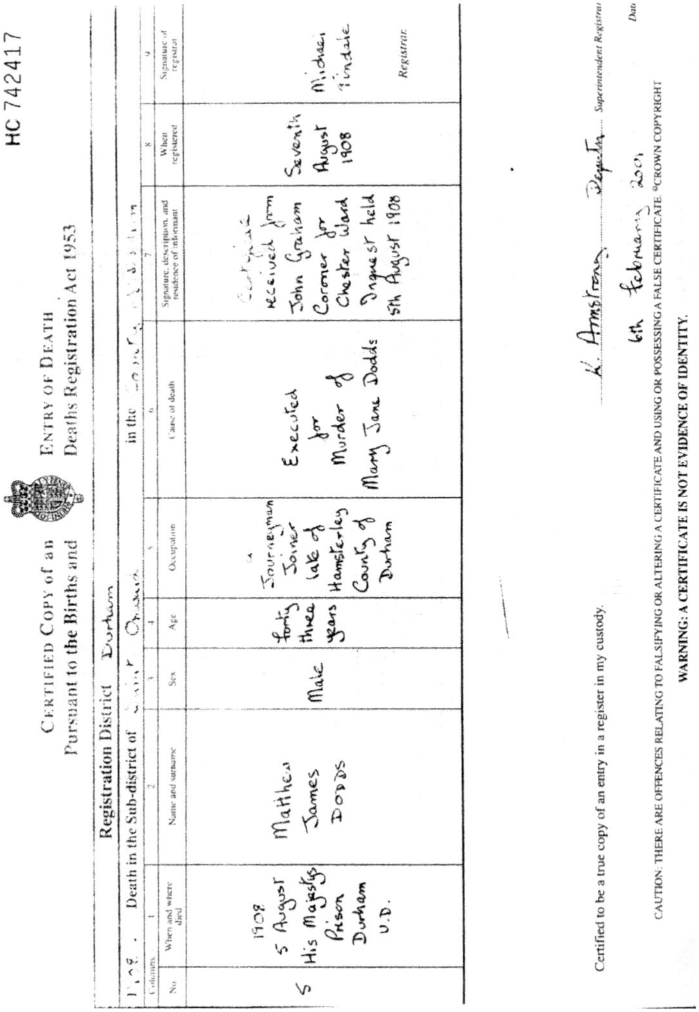

HC 742417

CERTIFIED COPY of an ENTRY OF DEATH

Pursuant to the Births and Deaths Registration Act 1953

Registration District Durham

19[illegible]. Death in the Sub-district of [illegible] in the [illegible]

No.	When and where died	Name and surname	Sex	Age	Occupation	Cause of death	Signature, description, and residence of informant	When registered	Signature of registrar
5	1908 5 August His Majesty's Prison Durham U.D.	Matthew James Dodds	Male	forty three years	Journeyman Joiner late of Hamsterley Hamsterley County of Durham	Executed for Murder of Mary Jane Dodds	Certificate received from John Graham Coroner for Chester Ward Inquest held 5th August 1908	Seventh August 1908	Michael Tindale Registrar

Certified to be a true copy of an entry in a register in my custody.

K. Armstrong Deputy Superintendent Registrar

6th February 2001 Date

CAUTION: THERE ARE OFFENCES RELATING TO FALSIFYING OR ALTERING A CERTIFICATE AND USING OR POSSESSING A FALSE CERTIFICATE. ©CROWN COPYRIGHT

WARNING: A CERTIFICATE IS NOT EVIDENCE OF IDENTITY.

Death certificate of Matthew James Dodds.

Rex -v- Matthew Jas. Dodds.

On the 20th February 1908. Mary Jane Dodds was murdered at her home at Hamsterley. Her husband the above named stated that went he went out of the house deceased was sitting in front of the fire the worse of drink -. He further alleged that she had fallen on the fire & burned to death. She was buried in the usual way. Later, as a result of a Doctor's finding an exhumation was ordered, and as a result the above named was arrested. Deceased having been beaten and strangled

At Durham Assizes on 1st July 1908, before Mr Justice Grantham sentenced to death.

Hanged 5th August 1908.
Executioners. H.A. & T.W. Pierrepoint.

Copy of entry in Official register of Murders retained at Durham Constabulary Headquarters.

Sources

UK Census Records 1841-1901
Registry of Births, Marriages and Deaths
Parish Registers for Hamsterley, St. James
Registers for Hamsterley Baptist Church
The Northern Echo Archive
The Teesdale Mercury Archive
The Auckland Times
Durham Constabulary
"Durham Executions, The Twentieth Century" by Maureen Anderson
"Hanged at Durham" by Steve Fielding
"Life in the Northern Dales" by Frank Sanderson
"The Durham Village Book" by Durham Federation of Women's Institutes

Printed in Great Britain
by Amazon

87772382R00120